SPLIT

GATE CLUB BOOK 3 -A NOVELLA

MARIE BOOTH

Thank you to all my author friends who cheered me on, but particularly K. W., who kept me focused and supported me during my darker, panicky moments.
You are a friend for the ages and I am honored to call you one of mine.

1

BLAKE

Anya's body twisted in rhythm as she whipped her head with every quick spin and smiled her lovely smile so every judge would mark us high.

I concentrated on the movement of my hips, the quickness of my legs and feet, the flow in the movement of my arms, the posture that marked me as one of the top salsa dance partners in the world.

We'd won the last two national competitions, but the IBDC in Sydney was like roping a star in the sky for ballroom.

The lifts I'd choreographed were complicated, yet we'd worked them for many months to make them look easy to anyone who didn't know the strength, balance and precision required. The competition was in three weeks and we'd already booked our flights and hotel and even shipped our costumes.

Nikki, our coach, a slim, petite woman, smiled when we finished. "*Bella*, Anya, dear." But watch your footwork in the quickest section."

"Oh yes, thank you. I will."

Nikki turned to me. "You're tilting your head too much on the second refrain. You mustn't lose focus simply because you enjoy the music." She laughed and we joined in. She squeezed my shoulder. "The lifts you created are spectacular and that section near the end stands out. "*Bueno*, Blake."

"Thanks, coach."

She sighed with pleasure and took a step back. "You're ready."

We thanked Nikki over and over for all the time and effort she'd put into coaching us. Before leaving the studio, she forced us to vow to get to the airport three hours ahead of time for our flight to Sydney.

As soon as the door shut behind Nikki, Anya jumped into my arms. I swung her around, then changed tactics and kissed her hard and fast. We couldn't stop smiling or kissing or talking about our trip just two days from now.

An hour later we showered and ate take-out Chinese food in my apartment, our bodies buzzing with adrenalin, hunger and lust as if we'd fought a battle. Despite dire warnings from Nikki about keeping our personal lives separate, we agreed our dancing had improved since we'd become lovers. Anya and I were more in sync than ever, more focused, more connected.

It wasn't unusual. Dancing was a sensual, sweaty, intimate experience. Many dance partners slid between the sheets in their rare time off.

She was demanding that night, not interested at all in slow seductions or extended foreplay. Five minutes after finishing our moo shu crab and spicy General Tso's chicken dish I was inside Anya's perfect body whispering dirty words that made her wet, sweet phrases that had her laughing, soft promises of how we'd win the competition.

"I love you." And I did, with every beat of my heart.

Her smile was brilliant, her excitement electrifying the room. Our dream was coming true after years of excruciatingly hard work. "Let's go out and celebrate," she said, holding up a black number she kept in my closet. Low in the back and short on the bottom, it showed off her gorgeous body to perfection.

"Tonight should be an early one." My practical side always kicked in when it came to sleep, food and scheduling rehearsals. Anya tended to let me organize her life, as long as the results worked out.

"You're too serious, Blake. Loosen up. I heard about a great club that just opened in Oakland. Let's go. I'm too wound up to sleep."

"If I didn't have to be in Marin tonight, I'd wear you out until you begged me to let you sleep."

"Mmm. Can we do that instead? Your mommy won't mind if we have a sleep over."

I had early classes at UC tomorrow. Dancing was my passion, but careers ended early and I was hoping to one day make a name for myself in the family law firm. From the time my dad came to parent's day at school and talked about how he helped people, I'd always known I wanted to work with my parents.

Although they'd danced ballroom themselves and had encouraged me along the way, it was their work that had always fascinated me. As lawyers they took on cases often overlooked or refused by other firms. The East Bay Community benefitted every day from their help and I wanted to be a part of that.

"When the competition is over, we'll take a few weeks off, find a resort with a beach and relax."

"And go to clubs?"

She'd never pass up an opportunity to dance. "Sure."

"You and me?"

"You and me."

She sighed, kissed my cheek and swayed as she walked toward the door, now dressed in skin tight jeans, a colorful silky blouse and her favorite red jacket. "Fine." She turned and held out her hand. "Walk me to the train."

We shared another few kisses on the way, then said goodnight. We'd planned to have one last rehearsal tomorrow afternoon, then head to our respective apartments to finish packing.

Because of an accident on the highway, I got to my parents' house later than usual. Although I had my own apartment in the city, their house was much more convenient to Berkeley and allowed me the ability to avoid the horrors of rush hour. Usually.

My seventeen year old sister, Val, was waiting for me.

"Can I use your car? Mine's in the shop."

I glanced at my phone to catch the time. Eleven p.m. Anya had texted she'd arrived home safe and sound. "No."

"Why?"

"It's a powerful machine and you don't have enough time on the road."

"But I have a party in Larkspur."

"Definitely no. Take the hybrid."

"That's Mom's car."

"It's only a year old and it runs great."

"But I want the Porsche. My friends aren't gonna want to show up at this classy party in a dumpy hybrid."

"You shouldn't be driving a bunch of your friends around. How many?"

"Two. Maddie and Crystal. Can't you take Mom's car?"

"I'm taking the train to school tomorrow." Her scowl was

legendary. "When you're twenty-one I might think about lending you the Porsche."

She pulled out her phone. "Fuck you, Blake." Turning away, she stormed up the stairs in seventeen-year-old Valeria fashion. "Yeah, it's a no go. He's a douche," she announced to whatever friend was on the phone.

"Love you too, Shorty." Petite like Mom, Val hated it when I called her that, but she deserved it. Little brat.

Yawning, I emptied my pockets, dumping my keychain in the china dish on the table near the front door. Wincing when I bent down to lift my dance bag, I flexed my shoulders, still a little sore from the work out. Heat would help, so I changed into a swimsuit and slid into the hot tub.

Closing my eyes, I allowed my mind to roam the enticing planes of Anya's body as my mouth and hands had a few hours earlier. Passionate perfection, whether on the dance floor or straddling my thighs. Sex was a stress reliever after a long hard rehearsal, but Anya was so much more than simply a sexual partner.

She was my future, damn my own career. I'd follow her to the ends of the planet and beyond, whether I worked as a dancer or a waiter or a lawyer like my parents. I had to end the day in her bed, her head on my chest, her soft breaths blending with mine.

Performing was great, especially when you won the title you'd worked so hard for, but my adrenaline rush took hold when Anya was beside me.

I toweled off and slid naked under the sheets. I had a class at UC Berkeley tomorrow at noon. At three thirty we were scheduled for our last rehearsal before the competition. I set my phone for five a.m. I'd go for a short run before breakfast, then make it to class with time to spare.

But it was dark when I woke up next. Someone was

ringing the doorbell. Dad went to answer it. I glanced at the clock. Three a.m.

Dad called out for mom in Spanish, his voice breaking. I pulled on a pair of shorts and took the stairs two at a time.

~

Present Time:

TOWELING SWEAT OFF MY FACE, I hit end on my phone to stop the music. The choreography was still in its planning stages. Warm bodies in the studio to work the routines would make all the difference. Still, Vic's rhythmic, heart pounding music was making the process easy, and I was pretty sure Popup911 was going to love what I'd done with the tunes he'd be using on his first national tour.

Vic had done me a solid and introduced me to his client. The kid, real name Keith Bishop, had been open minded about checking out what I could do. I recorded a video to one of Victor's songs, standing in for P and using a few dancer friends as chorus. He called me five minutes after I sent him the video, practically bursting a gut with excitement. He told me later he'd watched the secret video another ten times. He even showed up just as I was closing to go over the moves face to face.

He was a natural dancer with a voice that could melt butter. Plus he was good looking and already had over a million followers on twitter. The Popup911 Tour was gonna break some attendance records.

This was my first big break as a choreographer. Yesterday I got a call from an agent who represented several touring groups and singles. Keith had recommended me and the agent was anxious to see my work. I sent him a few videos and he called back, asking me to fly to LA, expenses paid. Some of the artists wanted to meet with me. I told him I had other commitments I couldn't break right now but could probably schedule a meeting in two weeks. He didn't seem at all put off.

No way was I letting my classes down. We had a recital coming up and the kids were...well they were gonna blow some minds, that's for sure.

I grabbed a quick shower in the studio locker room before dressing in dark jeans, a black button down, boots and the leather jacket Val had gotten me for my last birthday. She always had great taste in clothes and enjoyed buying me shit online. Amazingly everything fit and looked great. Even worse, she scolded me when I ran into a department store even to buy socks and boxer briefs.

I had to set her straight. My sister should not be buying my underwear. End of story. Only taking care of me made her happy and I would do whatever I could to give her every ounce of joy she could squeeze out of life.

I did a walk-through of the studio, shutting down lights and reassuring myself that everything was where it belonged. I locked the front door and turned toward the restaurant.

A woman stared at me from across the street. A woman I thought I'd never see again. I raised my hand and started to call out, but she turned away and headed down the stairs to BART and Muni. In a daze, I stepped off the curb, but the sound of a car horn had me jumping back. Traffic was too heavy in this spot, so I raced to the corner and waited for the light to change. I took the stairs two at a time, but when I got to the station lobby, I had no idea which way she'd gone.

Could it really be Anya, or was she on my mind because

I'd been dreaming about her lately? It could have been anyone, but I'd stay watchful.

I smiled, my chest warming with a chance to make things right between us. Tiny threads of hope wove together in a slow dance. I was a sap to think she'd ever forgive me.

2

ANYA

"How did you feel when Jim called you a name?

"You mean when he called me a dumbass shit eater?" The thirteen year old boy glared at me. "How do ya think?"

"Put it into words."

"Pissed off. Fucking mad."

"I'd like you to make an effort to try to think of other more appropriate words to describe your feelings. Words you might have used in front of your parents. You're a smart young man. Use your brain."

He smirked, obviously trying to get a rise out of me. "Hella pissed?"

"Try harder." I had to bite my lip to keep from laughing. Billy was testing me. Breaking into a fit of giggles would not encourage him to speak to people with respect.

"Angry. Steamed."

"Excellent."

"I was angry enough to kick him in the balls."

I let it go. "Did you?"

"Did I what?"

He wanted to hear me say it. "Kick him in the scrotum."

"No. Or the balls either."

"Did you take any action at all?" I asked.

"Yeaaaah." Said using the *duh* tone.

"And..."

"He didn't like it one bit."

"What did you do?"

"You have the report right there." He folded his arms and scowled.

The school had sent me a copy of the investigation they'd made before suspending him for two weeks. "I want to hear your version of what happened."

"I took his phone from his bag during gym, scrolled through his photos, found one of his dick pics and sent it out to his contacts."

"Only the picture?"

"I might have written a couple of words. That's all."

I waited.

"Pitiful. Scrawny."

"How old is Jim?"

"Thirteen."

A thirteen year old kid had a picture of his penis on his phone. The mind reels. "Was your response appropriate?"

"You'll say no."

"What do you say?"

"I'll say no if it gets me outta your office."

Bright, funny, smartass kid. I liked him. I'd only had time to skim through his file, but he'd been through the ringer over the last year. His parents died four years ago in an accident. Two years later, the foster parents he'd adored were shot down during a convenience store robbery. Now he lived with his paternal grandmother, a woman in her mid-seventies. According to the report, Billy and Mrs. Stanton did not always get along well.

Raising a thirteen year old boy after losing a son and daughter-in-law would be difficult on many levels.

"How well do you know Jim?" I asked.

"No one knows him. No one likes him. He's always by himself talkin' sh...crap about everyone."

"He's done this kind of thing with other kids in your class?"

"Yeah."

"How do they respond?"

"Another kid punched him when Jim called him a pussy. That kid got suspended for a week. Jim never gets in trouble cause he's gimpy."

"That's inappropriate. Try harder, please."

"He has a limp. One leg's shorter than the other."

I clamped down on my wince. Billy had never seen me walk with my cane. My secretary let him into the office when I was already at my desk. I didn't feel it was necessary to distract my clients with my own disability. I was luckier than most. I could have broken my neck when I fell. I swallowed hard and asked another question.

"What do most of the children in your class do when he calls them names?"

"Some of them call him names back. Most walk away."

"What do you think you might have done that would have kept you out of my office?"

"Ignore the asshole."

"Try..."

"I know, I know." He rolled his eyes. "Ignore what he says."

"What else?"

"I dunno."

"Think about it."

"For how long?"

"Until our next session."

"I haveta come back, Ms. Vetrova?"

"Twice a week."

"All 'cause of a dick pic?"

"That and other things."

He stared down at his hands. "I can tell ya why I sent the picture."

"I'm listening."

"He said I was dumb, but I'm the smartest kid in the class. He's the dork."

"Are you referring to his intelligence?"

"Isn't that what dork means?" He didn't look too sure.

"When you come in next time, please bring a list of words you can use in a normal conversation other than dork, gimp, shit, fuck, crap and asshole. I'd also like to hear your ideas on how you might have dealt with this incident in a different way."

"You're givin' me homework? There's only three more weeks of school and I'm suspended for two of them."

"Yes. I'm assigning homework."

"Jeez."

"Is your grandmother here?"

"Yeah. She's taking me to class now."

"What kind of classes are you taking?" I asked, inserting the report back into its folder.

"Dance."

I stilled. "In the neighborhood?"

"Yeah. Around the corner."

I knew exactly where the studio was. I'd lurked nearby for weeks after I'd seen him drive past in that SUV with the silly vanity plate, *MRDANCY.* It was so Blake.

"You take dance?" Too late, I glanced at Billy's chair, the chair he had to be strapped into because a drunk driver hit him when he was riding his bike. He may never walk, although his Gram says the doctors are hopeful. He'd gone through several procedures at Stanford Children's Hospital, but so far…

Right now, his smile was ear to ear as he rattled off information. "Yeah, my teacher choreographs dances for me and Sammi, she's in a wheelchair too, and you wouldn't believe what this other kid Dwayne can do. He's only got one real leg but he can do that popping stuff and even some krump moves."

"Sounds great."

"Yeah, our teacher picks awesome music: hip hop and bluesy stuff and Broadway, 'cept I hate the pop crap."

"Try harder."

He grunted, completely annoyed with me and my requests. "I don't like pop music."

"He plays that too?"

"Yeah, he's got a friend who writes a little bit of everything for a lot of the big names on the charts. It's cool. They're best buds and my teacher says we can meet him one day."

Victor. It had to be Victor. "What's your teacher's name?" I had to hear it for myself.

"Mr. Enfield. Blake."

"Blake." The sharp stab remorse that came with the memory surprised me. "Is he a good teacher?"

"Yeah, but he sweats a lot."

"All dancers sweat when they're doing it right."

"Yeah? Do you know some dancers?"

"I used to."

"His studio's really close, next to that Italian restaurant

where you can get the biggest plate of spaghetti and meatballs in the world. Grams is taking me when my suspension is over if I *behave* myself." He rolled his eyes then gave me a scrutinizing stare. "You know him?"

"I might." I knew where the studio was. I'd been lurking nearby for weeks. Ever since I'd unexpectedly seen Blake teaching a class through the window of his studio.

"Says he used to be a lawyer. I think he's rich as that Amazon dude."

"Not likely. Why do you think he's rich?"

"He drives a Tesla."

"Teslas are pretty common in northern California."

"I guess. We don't have a car. Gram doesn't drive anyway."

"You take the train to get here?"

"Yeah." He sat up a little straighter, his smile brightening. "You wanna come to my recital?"

This time he'd really shocked me. "You...put on a recital?"

"Yeah. In two weekends on a Sunday. You won't believe how cool it is."

"I..."

"Great. I'll getcha a ticket."

"Oh, Billy... I don't think..."

"Oh." His face fell. "It's okay. Never mind. We're not really dancing."

"Sure you are. You're moving to music. That's dancing." The kid looked crushed. "It's at the studio?" He nodded. "I'll come, but I'll probably just stand in the back. That okay?"

"Sure." He grinned again and I quashed down my misgivings. "Gram says dancing is good for the soul."

"It is. I'll get my own ticket."

"We get four free tickets and it's just Gram coming."

"Oh. Then thank you. I'd like a ticket."

"Yes!" He pumped his hand in the air.

I never imagined I'd be smiling when I thought about seeing Blake again. Maybe speaking to him. "But I'll only come if you arrive on time to our sessions and do your homework, including the homework you're required to do during your suspension."

"Okay." He didn't look so happy now.

"And when you go back to school I want you to talk to Jim. Try to get to know him."

"What?"

"Maybe he needs a friend."

"Maybe he needs a kick in the..."

I arched a brow.

"Behind. I was gonna say behind."

"Mmm hmm. Our time's up. I'll see you on Tuesday."

"Goodbye, Ms. Vetrova."

With practiced ease he spun the chair and wheeled it toward the door. Wheelchairs on a dance floor? Blake had always thought outside the box when it came to dance, but this was something... Something wonderful.

The familiar warmth in my chest surprised me. I shook it off and thought about how it would be to run into the man who'd haunted my dreams for almost eleven years.

Blake had seen me yesterday. I hadn't meant for that to happen, but he'd recognized me immediately. Fortunately, I'd been at the top of the stairs that led to the train station.

Had he tried to come after me? Probably not.

I pushed away my sadness and wrote up my notes on Billy's session.

3

BLAKE

The kids' rehearsal went better than expected. Billy was upbeat, despite the trouble he'd gotten into at school. His partner, Sammi, fed off Billy's energy. That was often the case with dance partners. One might have slept poorly or had a bad day and the other partner's energy would pick them up. Help them focus and reignite.

The adult class was scheduled for 7:30, so I shut down the lights, flipped the sign, locked the studio and walked next door to Bel Cielo, my all-time favorite Italian restaurant. I was a regular. Well, more than a regular. I'd gone to school with Chef Sloane's husband, Vic, a composer for many of the latest stars on the charts.

He'd been a dark horse for so long, involved in shady dealings with his dad, trying to drag Damien in as well. But he'd found his footing when his dad was arrested and he had to man up and take responsibility. He threw his mind and spirit into his music, and what was coming out of that recording studio today was on everyone's playlists, including mine.

My stomach rumbled and saliva flowed with the first

whiff as I opened the door. The food was awesome and usually free, as long as I promised Sloane I'd tip the server and the bartender generously. Sloane treated her staff like family and woe to the poor soul who mistreated them. Those kitchen knives were sharp, and gelding was not an unreasonable punishment in Sloane Gabrielli Hanley's estimation.

She and Vic had lined up another group sail on their catamaran for this weekend. Dame and Cassie would be there along with Rachel, the Gate Club's annoying as shit secretary and her fiancé, Marley, another guy I knew from school. He used to hide in the research section of the library, studying up on endangered species or the effects of greenhouse gasses on the environment. Compared to Dame, Vic and me, he was on the scrawny side, so we'd made sure the resident bullies kept their hands off him.

Marley had been a quiet, serious kid. How he'd hooked up with Rachel was still a mystery.

"Is there any chance I can get a window seat today?"

Gio, the maître 'd, folded his arms and frowned. "Say please."

"Please." One didn't argue with Gio. He was the boss out on the floor and I did whatever I could to stay on his good side.

Although he was part Roma, the scowl was only a mask. We got along pretty well, considering he was uber protective of Sloane and the rest of the staff. I might have put on the charm with one or two of the servers, but Gio would have cursed me in some spooky way and I'd have probably broken out in zits and hives the next day.

The staff was off limits. I could live with that.

Right now, another female was occupying my thoughts. The chance to catch a glimpse of Anya was the main reason

I wanted a window seat. But the vision of my former partner turning away and running down the stairs dissolved the moment Chef Sloane slipped a steaming hot plate of lasagna in front of me. She smiled at my grateful expression.

Oh, the fuck yeah.

I'd called in my order ahead of time, but on Wednesdays lasagna was one of the specials and I almost always chose it. Marie, my parents' Italian cook, had made it my favorite meal growing up, but Sloane's was even better.

Sloane sat across from me as I sprinkled cheese on top. She glanced at the empty chair. "Where's Joan?"

"She dumped me three weeks ago."

"So soon? Was that a record?"

"No. I think Jess was a record. Only took a few hours."

"Ouch."

I shoveled in a forkful then grunted in pain, downing a few sips of water. "Hot."

"Do you see the steam? You do this every time you order it. Lasagna is supposed to be served hot. The diner waits patiently for it to cool."

"Yours is dangerously hot. Third degree lasagna burns would be a bad way to go."

"Might keep you from chatting up the staff."

"Did I say a word? One word?"

"Not today."

"I will take an oath if necessary, mama bear."

"I keep my cleaver sharp. That's all you need to know."

"Message received."

We grinned at each other and I lifted my fork, blowing on it dramatically, then swallowing the cheesy deliciousness of Bel Cielo lasagna. "Mmmmmmm."

"So what's with you wanting the window seat? You're usually happiest in the corner."

"No reason." I glanced away.

"You're a terrible liar."

I shrugged. Sloane stared. I sighed. "I thought I saw her yesterday."

"Her who?"

"Someone from my past."

"Someone you liked?"

"More than liked."

"How long ago?" she asked, leaning forward, all attention on me.

"She was twenty. I was twenty-one."

"Ten years? And you haven't kept in touch?"

"Didn't have the balls to try."

"If you see her again, will you speak to her?"

"She'll turn around and run the other way. I did a horribly stupid thing when we were together. Ruined her life."

"Apparently not if you saw her walking around town. How did she look?"

"As beautiful as ever."

"Healthy?"

"From what I could see."

"Well dressed?"

"Professional."

"Then I think you can cut the self-pity party."

I'd lifted my hand to indicate to the bartender I wanted a drink. A minute later my straight up high-end tequila was on the table.

"Blake..."

"Shush. I'm wallowing. Give me a minute." I downed the shot, then frowned. "I'd take the bottle but I'm teaching later."

"So dramatic. You should've been an actor."

"Makeup gives me zits."

We sat in silence for a few minutes, my appetite waning. I stared out the window, part of me hoping for a glimpse of Anya's thick blonde hair, large eyes and perfect ass. And what would I do? Follow her to see where she lives? She must be married by now. Probably has kids. Would she even want to talk to me?

"Invite her here for dinner. Sometimes a face to face talk in a relaxing environment is the best thing." I didn't respond. "Vic and I knew each other in college."

"Yeah, he told me. But he saved you from a couple of drunk frat boys, right? Not exactly the same situation."

"Doesn't hurt to try to patch things up."

"Would you want to be with the guy who dropped you during a rehearsal? Who injured you so badly you could never compete again?"

"Shit."

"Yeah. Shit."

"But it was an accident, right?"

"I wasn't in a good place. Hadn't slept. My mind was somewhere else. I should have cancelled the rehearsal." I didn't want to drag out the gory details.

"Oh, Blake." Sloan covered my hand with hers and squeezed gently. "I'm sorry that happened. Must have been awful for both of you. But people have a huge capacity to forgive. If you see her, give her a chance."

"Thanks, but..."

She held up her hands in surrender. "Okay. I'll leave you to your wallowing. Back to the kitchen for me. Stay as long as you like."

"I have a Salsa class to teach. Adult beginners. They're a fun group."

"Come by afterward."

"I'll probably head to my apartment. Long day." I'd spent most of it choreographing a video, this time for a local band that was starting to make some noise in the area. Vic had a lot of connections in the music world and there were few things I liked better than putting movement to music.

"Okay, but you know you're always welcome."

She kissed me on the cheek and I asked my server to pack up my lasagna. I'd eat it after class.

As I turned the key in the lock of my studio door, a reflection in the window caught my eye. A woman, her red coat lapels turned up, a knit hat hiding her hair. I spun around, but a group passed where she'd been standing and she was gone when they'd finally cleared out.

She'd been looking at the studio.

"Hey, teach!" One of my students had arrived. "Are you okay?" He followed my gaze, but like me, there was nothing to see. Just the usual seven p.m. weekday foot traffic and the occasional homeless man or woman.

"It's nothing." I turned to Clive. "Have you been practicing?"

"Yep. My downstairs neighbor complained." He laughed.

"You can practice here if you want." He and his fiancé wanted to do something special at their wedding, so I choreographed a fun number. They were already students, so I didn't charge. Weddings were expensive enough.

I gestured him inside and searched the crowd one last time for the woman in the red coat.

4

ANYA

"I can't deal with this. I just can't." Ms. Nelson rose from her chair. We still had another ten minutes left to the session.

"We have more time."

She sighed and sat, turning away to look out the window.

"When was the last time you spoke to your sister?"

"We haven't spoken since mom's funeral." She looked up at me. "I'm not being unreasonable. I mean, I knew it was hard for her to care for Mom. She's got little kids and Mom needed a lot of extra help, but she didn't even talk to me about it. She sent Mom to assisted living and three months later, our mother was dead."

"You told me the doctors said she would have died no matter where she was."

"I know, I know, but she never... My sister never seemed to need Mom the way I did. Mom and I used to talk every day on the phone after I moved out. "Jenny is a stay-at-home Mom. I work sixty hour weeks. I couldn't have... I couldn't..."

My client seemed to be wasting away before my eyes. Surviving on guilt and anger, eating her up from the inside out. I knew that recipe.

She and her sister Jenny needed each other more than ever.

"How often did you speak to your sister during that time?"

"Not often." She glanced down at her lap, her fingers clutching together. "I've been a bitch to her."

"No one is at fault in this situation, but if you two could meet, talk with an open heart, it might help."

"Do you think she'll forgive me?"

"I don't know your sister, but I believe forgiveness brings a kind of grace, and you two deserve that after all you've been through."

Those words caught in my throat as I thought of all the anger I've been carrying around, even after all this time.

Ms. Nelson glanced up at me, tears streaking her cheeks. "I want to forgive her. And myself. Can you help me? Us?"

"Yes, if you both want it. Talk to her. See if she'll come with you to your next appointment."

She was smiling as she left the office, hope in her eyes where before there had only been anger. It felt good to help a client find some relief.

If only I could help myself.

After Billy's last appointment I'd been sneaking glances at the dance studio on a regular basis. Blake had almost seen me again, but a group of office workers blocked his view. I'd joined them and split off at the corner. Headed here for my appointment.

I locked up, took the utilitarian cane down from its hook on the wall, and made my way to BART, hoping the after rush hour train would be a little less crowded. Halting in front of the Italian restaurant I passed every evening, I toyed with the idea of getting take-out. My cupboards were pretty bare at my little house and a relaxing meal might take my mind off my clients and focused more on the following week and the short vacation I'd planned.

Loud chatter broke my train of thought. I turned to see a group of happy couples exiting the dance studio next door.

Crap.

I ducked into the restaurant. The absolute last person I wanted to see right now was Blake Enfield.

Unfortunately, the place was hopping. The host, a cute young man with a serious expression, told me the wait would be forty-five minutes.

"Can I eat at the bar?" I'd ditched the idea of getting take out, even if it meant I'd be traveling on BART and Caltrain at a later hour than I usually liked.

"Of course, Signora." He led me to a seat near the end of the bar. "I'll bring over a menu in a moment."

"Thank you."

"Can I get you anything to drink?" The bartender had a smile that probably had men buzzing around her all evening. Or women.

"I'll let you know after I decide what I'm eating."

"Take your time. No rush at all. Water?"

"Yes, please." California restaurants usually asked before serving water. Too many years of drought had kept our population on the conservative side.

After reading the specials, I fell back on an old time favorite and ordered the chicken parm, switching the side of pasta for an order of sautéed asparagus. The days of asking for no cheese were long gone.

Female dancers who worked with partners tasked with lifting them, couldn't add any extra pounds to our already slim frames. These days I didn't have a guy to kiss let alone someone to lift me up. Cheese had become my favorite comfort food.

I'd filled out, but not to the point of feeling I had to watch calories. I'd actually grown breasts, which was nice, although there was no one around to admire them. Or do other things to them.

Since I'd seen Blake again, my mind had been leading my body down a path of sexual frustration. He was still so beautiful. Impossible to ignore, even in my dreams. I'd been waking up wet and achy.

"Anya?"

A shiver sent icy fingers down my spine, my primal brain kicking in big time. The man's voice was way too familiar.

Stay and face him or ask for my food to be packed up and leave...the more civilized version of fight or flight.

Leave, leave, leave, my heart screamed, but bumping into him was bound to happen at some point or another. My new office was around the corner and I was so proud of having built up my business enough to afford the space. No, the restaurant was a public place, in it's odd way a perfect place to meet again for the first time. I'd get this over with and that would be that.

I turned and my breath deserted me.

Blake had always been a good looking guy, but we'd been young when I'd seen him last. Now, at just past thirty, he'd filled out in all the right ways, his face a beautiful melding of his mixed heritage. High cheekbones, full lips, skin that glowed warmly despite the low lighting in the restaurant and dark brown eyes that had always made me feel like I was home.

"Blake." I didn't pretend I was surprised to see him. These days I rarely bothered to dissemble. Plain facts were the quickest way to a satisfying conclusion. The seat beside me was vacant. "Do you have time to sit and talk?"

His worried gaze disappeared, relief washing across his features. Blake had always been an open book with his emotions, a fact which had haunted me for a lot of years.

I should have seen. I should have known something was up when he came to our last rehearsal. But I'd been blinded by the excitement of our upcoming international competition. I hadn't wanted to look deeper. To ask questions.

"You ordering too, Blake?" the bartender asked as Blake slid into the seat. "Not that I want to discourage you from stuffing yourself but I'm pretty sure I saw you eating lasagna by the window a few hours ago."

"I'll have an espresso and a tiramisu."

"Anisette for the espresso?"

He nodded. "Thanks."

Raising my hand to get the bartender's attention, I noticed it was shaking slightly. A drink might steady my nerves. "I'll have a glass of sauvignon, please."

"Coming up."

I turned on the bar stool to face my former lover.

5

BLAKE

"It's so great to see you again, Anya. What brought you into the city? Are you working nearby?"

I hated small talk, but I couldn't see any way around it. I wasn't ready to poke at the elephant in the room.

"I share office space with a colleague. We each see clients two days a week. I work two days out of my home as well."

"Clients?"

"I'm a social worker."

My shoulders relaxed. "I can totally see you doing that. You used to be able to sense when something was wrong. To say the right thing to make it better."

She frowned and glanced at her hands, folded on the bar. "Half my clients are children. Working with them has changed my life in a lot of good ways." Her brow wrinkled. "I don't usually talk about my job with..."

"I hope you aren't going to say *strangers*."

She hesitated, then shook her head. "Never that. Too much history between us."

She glanced back at me just as the drinks came. We

sipped our respective beverages, the mood sloping downward at a quick pace.

"How about you?" she asked, then frowned. "I mean... I've seen you coming out of the studio. Congratulations. I know it was one of your dreams."

"Did you see the name?"

"Mr. Dancy Studios. Made me laugh."

"You always loved the Austen book and the movie."

"And you always tried to get me to say you were hotter than Mr. Darcy. That he probably couldn't even salsa."

We laughed, but only silence followed, awkward again.

"Did you get your law degree?" she asked.

I nodded. "I'm still a member of the bar, Still have a couple of clients but gave up most of my practice. Law didn't really satisfy the creative beast I carry around."

Her food came, but she continued to stroke the stem of her wine glass. I pointed at the chicken parm. "It'll get cold."

"You're the only person I know who doesn't mind burning his tongue." Her voice had grown little deeper. A little softer.

I smiled. "Yeah, that happens a lot. I probably have callouses. Which, ya know, might be a good thing."

I winked, hoping for a smile, but she glanced away, then snatched up her wine. "I'll take my chances and let it cool." She took a quick sip. Then another. I'd made her uncomfortable. I didn't want that.

"I'm sorry. I should leave. Let you eat."

She reached out to touch my hand, then pulled slowly away at the last minute. "No. Please stay."

Anya hadn't changed much physically. Blonde hair cut to just below shoulder length, bright blue eyes, an elegant neck I used to cover with kisses, and a gaze that could put you in your place without a word spoken. Even sitting on a bar stool her back was as straight as an Italian Cypress.

Dance training doesn't just up and go away when your career ends. Or when someone ends it for you.

Her coloring, posture and cool attitude had always made me think that somewhere in her DNA she must have been related to Russian royalty. My empress, I used to call her.

But tonight her nerves were showing.

I glanced at my bouncy knee. Mine too.

Cutting and spearing a piece of chicken, she examined the amount on her fork. Eating for Anya had always been an exercise in discipline, as it had for me during our years of competition and training. After a moment, the chicken disappeared into her mouth and I watched as she chewed and swallowed, not wanting to miss her expression.

She closed her eyes. "Mmm. This is very good." Another piece disappeared as quickly as the first.

"I'll introduce you to Chef Sloane. She's married to Victor Hanley. You remember Vic?"

"Yes. And Damien Granger. Two reprobates." She didn't say that with any animosity in her tone, but I'd kept her away from my two buddies, more because they would have hit on her than for any other reason.

"Both married and happy."

"Their wives must be strong women to keep those two in line."

I poured another dash of anisette into my espresso. "They are."

She glanced at my left hand. "No ring for you?"

I've never found anyone like you, I almost blurted out, then quickly swallowed a spoonful of my delicious dessert, deciding to avoid dangerous territory. "I'm hardly ever home. Always working. Doesn't make for domestic bliss."

"Your studio's in a good area," she said.

"My first was in the Richmond District, not far from the beach, but last year I moved into the space next door to Sloan's restaurant. Vic and Dame own the realty company that owns the building."

"So you three see each other often."

"Yeah. Their wives have learned to tolerate me." I said, smiling.

"Amazing. So you're happy?"

"The dance studio is everything I ever imagined." I caught a flash of regret in her eyes and started to apologize.

"It's okay. You can talk about dance around me. I won't collapse in a fit of tears."

"Anya..."

"No. We will not discuss what happened. Not today. Maybe not ever."

"I'm so sor..."

"Shush!"

Two of her fingers landed on my lips. I stayed completely still, hoping she'd leave them there. I wanted to grasp her wrist and suck those delicious fingers into my mouth, but they disappeared as her cheeks pinked up.

"We can talk about normal subjects. We can wave at each other in passing. We can even have dinner once in a while. But we cannot talk about that day."

Her hand rested on the bar, so I covered it with mine, giving it a gentle squeeze before releasing it. The fucking pain in her eyes tore me apart. "If I can see you once in a while, just as a friend, or even a former friend, I'll agree to anything you want. I've missed you."

"I've missed you too." She smiled tentatively. "I think I've been invited to one of your recitals. I have a client who's a student."

"Yeah, who?"

"Billy..."

"Billy Arthur? He's amazing. And he's great with the other kids"

"He is?"

"Yep, although it took a little time."

"Is the entire class made up of alternately abled children?"

"No, but it all gels. You'll see."

"I'm not surprised. You were a wonderful choreographer."

"Still am."

"And you remain so humble."

"I was born to dan... Damn it, I'm... I mean..." Uch. I was totally fucking up this conversation.

She smiled, but the warmth I remembered didn't touch her eyes. "I think I should head out."

"Just a sec." I waved at a couple of the servers and they came over. Gio trailed behind. "This is Anya. She works nearby and loves Italian food. She'll be back."

They crowded around and shook her hand as I introduced the annoying, yet loveable staff.

"Can you get her a take-out container?"

"It'll be a pain to carry on BART and Caltrain."

"Where do you live?"

"Palo Alto"

"What? In the sticks?" She grew up in the city.

"I'll have you know the City of Palo Alto is part of Silicon Valley and therefore not the sticks."

"Uh huh."

"I take clients at my home on Mondays and Tuesdays. Plus, I'm close to the hospital at Stanford. And my doctor."

She was seeing a doctor. Was she ill? Or was it related to her fall? "I'm driving you home," I said.

"You're not. You live in the city, right?"

"Yeah, but I'm all wound up from the rehearsal. Don't have to get up early either. I'm driving."

"Still ordering people around?" She fisted her hand in indignation. Same empress.

"Yep." said Gio.

"Yep," said Kara, Anya's server.

"Yep," said Julie, the bartender.

I frowned. "Get back to work before I tell Chef Sloane you're slacking off."

"We never see you in here with a girl," Gio said, looking Anya over.

"She's a woman, lunkhead," Julie scolded. "And she's way above your class, Blake."

"Don't I know it."

"Are you on a date?" asked Gio.

"No," Anya said.

"No," I said at the same time.

"You were holding her hand."

"We're old friends," Anya explained.

"He can't stop staring at you." Gio turned to me, grinning. "Might as well ask her out."

"Shoo. Now." I waved my arms and they left, laughing softly and sneaking peeks back in our direction.

"Don't pay any attention to them. Here. Open your mouth." I held out a heaping spoonful of tiramisu, her long ago favorite dessert.

"You're only encouraging them with this move."

I leaned forward and spoke softly. "Open wide."

"You're a devil." But she was eyeing the spoon.

"You want it. You know it. You want it soooo bad."

She snatched the spoon out of my hand and turned away before sliding it into her mouth. I frowned. She was taking away all my fun.

Watching Anya eat had always been one of my top five favorite activities. Especially when we shared a meal in bed. She'd denied her body food to hold onto her dancer's weight, but when we spent a day or a night or both making love, she'd sometimes indulged in her deepest culinary desires.

Other desires too. She'd liked how we played together.

I took back the spoon and scooped up another bit of creamy coffee flavored goodness, imagining spreading it on her nipples and licking it off.

My cock hardened at record speed, painful against the tight denim of my jeans. Man, his timing sucked.

6

ANYA

From the moment Blake slid onto the stool beside me, my traitorous body made it perfectly clear it would have preferred a delicious bite of Blake over the tiramisu.

He'd always been a charmer, had always gotten his way with me from the moment we acknowledged our attraction. Not that I hadn't been on board. But when the competition was only a few months out, we'd agreed to focus solely on the dances he'd choreographed, on the critiques from our very well paid instructor, on the rhythms and the styles and the connection we shared when we danced.

Each dance became a seduction, spurred on by our glorious music and Blake's amazing choreography. Gentle dips and turns as we tested and teased were soft kisses, feathery strokes. That perfect first discovery. Powerful twists and lifts showed the man's growing dominance and the woman's willing submission, only to be flipped on its head by quick turns out of his grasp, teasing and torturing until his movements turned pleading. The last lifts were always sensual, touching as much body surface as possible, a perfect union of partners. We ended wrapped as one, gazes locked, whispered words of love under imaginary soft cotton sheets.

I sighed and slid off the stool, using the edge of the bar to support some of my weight. Waving away Blake's black Amex, I handed the server my more mundane Visa, then snatched up my cane.

Blake's eyes widened.

"I'm fine on public transportation. I do it round trip two days a week and have never had a problem."

"I'm driving."

"I'm not in pain. I use the cane more for balance than anything else."

"My car is in the lot behind the restaurant. We can leave through the back door."

We stared at each other for what seemed like an eternity, neither of us wanting to cave. The server broke the spell when she handed back my card. I huffed through my nose. "If I ever see pity in your eyes. Or guilt. I will use this cane in an inappropriate way."

"Deal."

Being Blake, he had to introduce me to the entire kitchen staff on the way out. Chef Sloane, a very attractive blonde, gave him a hug and me a warm smile. She extended her hand and we shook. "So you're the mysterious Anya."

"Not so mysterious."

She glanced at the cane, then back at me, but didn't ask any questions. Maybe she already knew what had happened. Victor and Damien certainly knew. Sloane turned to Blake. "Behave, Mr. Enfield."

"I'm driving my lovely companion home. All the way to Palo Alto."

"You live in the sticks?"

"It's not the... I faced off against the critique. "Where do you live?"

"Marin."

"Oh, c'mon. Marin County is more the sticks than Palo Alto."

"Oh really?"

"What's the determining factor?"

"Decent restaurants."

"You're on, pick a cuisine."

Sloane narrowed her eyes. "French. Country style, not haute."

"I can think of three off the top of my head."

"Yes, but are they good?"

"Come as my guest. Friday night?" I asked. I had three day weekends.

"We're going sailing for the weekend. Why don't you join us?"

"I don't think..."

"We have plenty of room. Damien and Cassie are coming along with Rachel and Marley. Vic is taking *Adagio* up to Point Reyes National Park." She turned back to Blake and shook her heading, sighing. "Guess we'll have to invite you too."

"I've already been invited by Vic."

"I'll have to talk to him. I usually get first approval on all guest lists." Their grins were a mile wide. My ruff bristled. They were close friends. Maybe they'd been more.

And why did I care?

"*Adagio* is Vic's toy boat." Blake pointed out.

Men could be such dopes. Totally wrong tactic.

Sloane narrowed her eyes. "Umm hmm. He keeps saying that."

"To keep peace, I'll ask properly. May I attend the party,

Madame Hanley?" Blake bowed, showing his inborn dancer's grace.

"Good boy. But it's Madame Gabrielli-Hanley." They laughed and hugged, Sloane sliding a sideways glance in my direction. "I'm training Blake to heel, only it isn't really working out."

"Never worked for me either." Only I hadn't meant for that to slip out. Except with Blake I'd always joked around. What had happened to that side of me?

Sloane laughed. "I like her already. So will Cassie and Rachel."

This was getting out of control. Showing up at a boat party escorted by Blake was not on my to do list. "I'll have to think about it but thank you so much for the invitation."

"Just let Blake know."

"I will."

The kitchen door exited to a dark alley with an uneven cement walkway. Usually in this situation I'd pull out my small flashlight, but Blake offered me his arm.

"I'm good." Although falling would be a disaster, especially on a hard surface.

"I'm not letting you face plant on my watch."

I glanced up, shocked, then relieved by the comment.

He winced. "Fuck. Sorry. I shouldn't have said that."

"No. It's fine. Beats pity any day. Thanks." I took his arm. I'd learned not to let pride get in the way of common sense.

I glanced up as we traversed the alley. He seemed taller, but it had been more than ten years since I'd walked or danced beside him. Of course, it could be me. Despite my efforts to stop, I tended to hunch slightly when I walked, always staring at the ground to stave off disaster. My fall with Blake hadn't been the only one, or even the worst.

He opened the passenger door of his high tech car and

helped me in. Blake used to drive a beat up blue Ford pickup around Marin County when we were teens, deciding to spend his generous allowance on more important things like cd's with music he could dance to, musical videos with routines by famous dancers, and a good sound system. Although his family could have afforded to get him a much nicer car, they expected him to earn the money by working. Blake thought work was a waste of his time. He wanted to spend the time rehearsing and choreographing instead, so the only jobs he'd ever taken were as a dancer.

Now he wore one of those watches that cost half what most people made in a year. His clothes might be casual, but I'd bet money that every stitch was high end. His Cuban Grandmother, who he called Lita, had taken her wealth and cut out of Cuba before Castro came into full power. She'd been an amazing woman who knew how to work her ass off and put aside money for the future of her family.

Mom and I had barely scraped by.

I shook my head and stared out the window. Why was I rehashing all this shit? "Nice car. A little different than the Blue Beast."

"That old truck got us around pretty well." Blake's expression turned nostalgic for a moment. He huffed a laugh. "I guess you think my ride is ostentatious."

"Why do you think that?"

"You used to mock me when I showed up in new dance shoes."

"The old ones were perfectly good."

"My feet were always growing."

"So, the dance studio... How did you... Never mind. Not my business."

"No secret. I inherited some money when Lita passed. Damien turned me on to a few startup company investments that took off. I've been Victor's lawyer for more than eight years, negotiating contracts with the high and mighty of the music industry. He pays me way more than I'm worth. Vic's my only personal client now, although I've helped Dame and Vic get their latest partnership set up." Blake's expression turned a little sheepish. "I do love my toys."

"You always did. I saw you in an SUV the other day."

"Yeah. I like larger toys too."

I frowned and turned my gaze to one of the homeless encampments, a sad state of affairs in a city where one bedroom apartments cost millions and cars like Blake's were the norm. Blake's parents came from wealthy roots, meeting as successful professional dancers before they turned to law and social justice. Even as a child of eleven Blake had always looked perfectly turned out, the latest model phone in his dance bag, his shoes perfectly broken in and shined.

I used to imagine he had a valet who dressed him and ironed his clothes, until I was invited to his home. No servants other than a cleaning service that came twice a week. But when I stayed for dinner, we'd eaten steak or delicious dishes I couldn't pronounce. The dance studio in his basement had sprung maple flooring to protect his joints and a surround sound stereo system.

When I was ten and showed passion along with potential, my mom argued with my *sometimes dad* as I called him. In exchange for my lessons, Mom cleaned the dance studio. She scrounged for extra work on top of her teacher's assistant position, struggled to get me in the line of sight of the best trainers so I could have a chance at partnering with a boy of Blake's ability. I'd come to class with shoes someone had outgrown and dance apparel we found at Goodwill or the local discount store.

Thanks to my mom and a lot of financial aid and hard

work to get me through my BS and my Masters, I was comfortable now, but somehow Blake's car, fancy watch and confidence, brought back the shame and the vulnerability of those days. I'd kept it hidden fairly well at the time, but Blake had known, yet had never made me feel like I was less. He'd treated me as precious. The only man I'd ever trusted. The only man to make me feel safe.

"You were never one of my toys, Anya. You were...my reason." His tone had lowered, the resonance rumbling so deeply I almost felt it in my chest.

"Your reason?"

He grinned, dispelling the more serious mood in a flash. "I'll tell you about it sometime."

We slipped onto 101 South. Another thirty-five minutes to Palo Alto. Another thirty-five minutes of sitting inches away from this beautiful man without touching him.

"Still keeping a journal?" I asked.

It had been a game we played. He'd tell me what he wrote in his journal and I'd have to guess if he was lying or not. I usually guessed correctly, although if it had been a lie, he never told me what he'd really written. "No. I stopped when law school took over every aspect of my life."

"I thought you wanted to go on. To keep competing."

"Didn't work out." His gaze drifted to mine. "Wasn't the same."

I shivered and wrapped my arms around my body. Why was this still a trigger for me? This sad tale was ten fucking years ago. I had to let it go. For good. "People change." I cracked the window. He smelled too damn good. I needed fresh air.

"I can change the temp if you're cold or hot."

I hit the button to close it. "No. I'm fine."

Out of the blue he took my hand. "Anya, I have to tell you..."

"Please don't."

"Why?"

I pulled away and knotted my hands in my lap, biting back the answers. Because I dealt in other peoples' feelings and entombed my own. Because calmness was my constant daily goal and chaos my enemy. Because the nightmares brought on by my struggles to find myself again had finally faded away.

Because if Blake talked about that day, feelings I'd buried in the Marianna Trench would spring to life. We'd never discussed the reason for the accident, but today, stuffed into this eighty thousand dollar car, I might cross over the razor wire I'd constructed and lash out, throw my hard won balance out the window.

Only I didn't want to be that person. How many times had I told my clients forgiveness brought grace? Healing. Why couldn't I let it go?

Blake took an exit near the airport and pulled over. "Why are you stopping?" I glanced around. We still had another twenty minutes.

"You're crying."

"Shit." I fished in my bag and pulled out a travel pack of tissues. I didn't even care that my nose sounded like a fog horn when I blew it.

"I'm sorry. I'm an idiot. I hurt you so badly."

"This has nothing to do with you. I'm worried about a client."

"Uh huh."

"What?"

"You may not believe this, but I want to help."

"I know that."

And I know your tells." He looked a little smug.

"What tells?"

"I shouldn't *tell* you," he said.

"You should just shut up, Blake. I mean it." He was so irritating. And sweet.

He put us back on the highway. "I won't be stupid again."

"You're a man."

"Oh. Way to throw down the gauntlet. You used to enjoy my manly assets."

I laughed. "You're still such a goof ball. I'm sorry. I talk to clients all day and I'm talked out. That's all. Don't take it personally."

"Got it." His voice was soft. Familiar in a comforting way. I slid my hand along the pull down armrest, wondering if he'd reach for me.

He didn't.

We were silent until he took the University Avenue exit and I had to direct him to Emerson Street and the cottage I rented five blocks from the center of town.

When we pulled in front of my tiny house, he smiled. "You live like a munchkin?"

I looked him over. He had a hopeful expression. Least I could do, I guess. "It's the perfect size for me. Want to come in?"

He eyed the red door warily. "You sure I'll fit?"

"Positive. I'll make us some coffee."

"Caffeine still your answer to the world's problems?"

"As all intelligent people would attest."

"I'd love a mug."

I went about grinding the beans, then adding the grounds to the french press as the water heated. "Thank you for bringing me home. Public transportation isn't ideal and I'm a little tired tonight."

The kettle sang and I poured the water, leaving it to steep. I put a few chocolate chip cookies on a plate and laid it on the table. "Let's sit."

My kitchen table only sat four, but I ate alone almost every night. Blake eyed the wooden Ikea chair doubtfully. I glanced around, searching for Shyster. "My cat is usually begging for food when I come home. But then, she doesn't like strangers."

"I won't be here for long." He eyed the press.

"Go ahead."

He jumped up and poured for both of us. Coffee was almost always enjoyed black, a habit we'd formed running from rehearsals to classes.

He munched on a cookie.

"You still see a doctor?" He asked.

"Yes, but not because of the original injury. A bicyclist ran me down one afternoon when I crossed the street. I reinjured my knee and hit my ear and my head on the curb. Since then I've had balance issues. The surgeries have helped enormously but I get dizzy once in a while. The cane is more for that than my knee or hip."

"But you take public transportation?"

"Saves me a few bucks if I get off at Milbrae and hop on the BART. Plus I like to feel independent."

"But what if you get dizzy while you're on a platform? Or a staircase?"

I shook my head and scowled. "I can deal with whatever comes up. I've been doing it for years now. I'm not letting a little bit of dizziness ruin my life."

"But…"

"There are people living independent lives in wheelchairs. Walkers. People without sight or hearing. People who live with pain on a daily basis. I can get where I have to go just fine."

"Why don't you take a rideshare?"

"Do you know what a rideshare costs from Palo Alto to San Francisco?"

"Then…"

"You sound like my mom."

"Your mom's a good lady."

"So is yours."

"Yeah." He looked away, took in a deep breath and turned back. "I've missed you, Anya."

And what could I say that wouldn't turn the tiny match flame burning in my chest into a full out torch. I'd missed him too. So much, all my good dreams had featured Blake and his sleek, dark body doing all kinds of dirty, nasty, wicked things to mine. My subconscious had never carried my hurt like a shield, never built a shed to store my grudges, never stomped on the good memories, the perfect memories, with combat boots branded with the logo *Pride*.

"I've missed you too. A lot."

His eyes glittered with emotion. Blake pulled out a pen and a receipt from somewhere and turned me around, using my back as a desk. He scribbled on the paper, then handed it to me.

"Call me. I want your number."

I picked up my phone and tapped in the number. It rang with a tone that almost shocked the shit out of me.

"Do you remember?" he asked, taking my hand and tugging me a little closer.

It was a song Vic wrote for us to use in a number, but we'd always liked it too much. Some of the music we used lost its appeal after hours and hours of practice. This one had been our special song and the last time we'd made love we'd put it on repeat.

"Vic gave it to me. Made it a ringtone too."

"He gave you the song?"

"Yep. He could have made a bundle adding lyrics and selling it to one of his clients."

"Who else do you use it for?"

"It's for you now. Just you." His voice had deepened.

"Blake..."

His eyes shone with mischief, his crooked smile one I remembered well. A shiver ran from the base of my neck to my lower belly, sending *about time* messages to my pussy.

Fortunately, my pussy was not in charge.

I began to walk toward the door, suddenly realizing he still hadn't released my hand. But then I hadn't tried to pull away either. His was warm and large and felt right. He smelled so good and it had been years since I'd even thought about kissing a man.

Was I thinking about kissing Blake? No. I could not possibly be that stupid.

Only we were at the door and he was leaning closer and I was leaning closer. He tugged my hand behind his waist, snaked his other hand to my nape, and brushed his lips across mine. I sighed and closed my eyes.

Push him away. Push him away. Now. Right this minute.

His lips curled and he opened his mouth, releasing my hand and cradling my face. "Anya."

I was going to reply and pull away, only his mouth was back on mine and his tongue was doing all kinds of delicious, lovely things to my mouth. It was only fair I return the favor.

He moaned and broke the kiss.

My pussy was Irish step dancing, waving a banner proclaiming the dry spell was over.

Dream on, you slut.

"Come with me to the party on *Adagio*."

"That's not a good idea. Especially now."

"Why especially now?"

I licked my lips, tasting coffee and Blake. "You kissed me."

"I'm pretty sure you kissed me back."

"And I rest my case. We are never going there again. Friends. Maybe."

"Maybe?"

"Seventy percent chance."

His lips twitched at the corners. "Will you *think* about coming?"

I was so thinking about coming, but not the way he meant it. "I will. I promise."

"I'm calling you later."

"Don't. I'll be in bed."

"The perfect place."

I unlocked the door and pushed him out. "Go. And don't call me. I need my sleep."

"Do I follow the yellow brick road?"

"What?"

"To get home from the tiny munchkin house."

"Figure it out yourself."

"Maybe you should write down the directions. I might get lost in the bustling City of Palo Alto."

"Are you done?"

"For now. Oh, one more thing."

He moved like lightning, kissing then sucking on my lips. Heat spread into every erogenous crevice and onto every sensuous surface of my needy, weak, traitorous body.

"Goodnight," he whispered against my ear.

Blake strolled to the garish car, taking his time to show off the way his ass filled the skin tight jeans and how his shoulders fit in that soft leather jacket. His long strides slid across the grass, cement, and asphalt as if each surface were made of glass.

I went to bed naked, praying he'd call. The phone rang an hour later.

"Anya?"

"What do you want?" I couldn't sound too eager.

"What I want and what I'm calling about are two totally different things."

"Blake..."

"I'll behave. I got a text from Billy's grandmother so I called their house. He wants to take extra classes, only I don't have a spare minute to teach another class. I was wondering if you'd be interested in getting involved with my kids program?

"Are you asking me to teach a dance class?"

"It was Billy's idea. I happened to mention his therapist was a fabulous dancer and when I told him I couldn't take on another class, he begged me to ask you to fill in. I think he's crushing on you doc.

"Anyway, you're in town on Wednesdays, right? I'll add another class for Billy and his buddies and maybe you could handle my regular tots classes on Friday afternoons. They meet in the smallest studio. They're so eager and adorable. I love those little beans."

I had no words. What gave him the right to talk about my personal life with one of my clients? Who else had he discussed my past with? The staff at Bel Cielo? Damien and Vic definitely, so maybe their wives? Their secretary, Rachel?

"Anya?"

My hands trembled, sweat soaking my nape. A familiar ache spread from my chest to my belly as visions of dancing with Blake broke through the barriers I'd erected. I clenched at the hem of my tee shirt. "You had no right."

"What?"

"To talk about what happened. I explained I didn't want to discuss it. That means you shouldn't discuss it with anyone else."

"But I didn't talk about the accident. Only that you used to dance. That you might dance again."

My heart was thudding so hard his words turned nonsensical. "This is real life, Blake. People don't shatter bones, then pirouette across the floor. Two surgeries then three more after the bicyclist ran me over on his way to work. I was in the hospital for a month because of the concussion. You grew up in dreamland. You snapped your fingers and miracles happened. Most of us don't have that ability."

"I'm sorry..."

"I'm never going to fucking dance again!"

"Anya. I'm so sorry. I didn't mean to upset you."

"Don't call again. P...please." I was having trouble catching my breath "I mean it."

I ended the call then limped to the dresser, opening the top drawer and unscrewing the bottle of anti-anxiety meds I kept on hand. The prescription said one, but I only took a half. I hated the damn things. Hated that I was heading toward a full blown panic attack and if I didn't pop a dose, I was going to fall apart.

The nightmares would creep back if I didn't stay in control.

Blake had lost focus while performing a difficult lift and

dropped me during rehearsal. I'd shattered my knee, cracked my hip and broken my wrist. He'd called an ambulance and gotten me to the hospital, staying in the waiting area for days until I'd agreed to see him.

I'd called off sex two months before we were set to leave for Sydney, feeling it might help us conserve energy. He'd argued but agreed.

After the accident, another dancer, Olav, texted me he'd overheard Blake and Shannon talking about becoming partners. Shannon said he could do a lot better than partnering with the Russian slut. He'd kissed the bitch, then they'd jumped in a ride share together. Shannon had always had the hots for Blake.

Olav had even suggested Blake had dropped me on purpose so his buddy Shannon could win the competition, but I would never believe that. Blake would not have destroyed my career on purpose.

But he'd come to rehearsal, tired and pale. He should have told me he wasn't up to rehearsing. I would have been angry at first, but... If he'd kept his dick in his pants and gotten some sleep the night before our last rehearsal, I might be dancing with a troupe, or teaching dance in a top class studio. Not hobbling around San Francisco.

I paced the bedroom, living room, kitchen. Dusted the book shelves. Shyster had crawled out of his hiding spot so I fed him. When he finished he cleaned his fur, then watched me.

Crazy human, right?

But I couldn't settle. My heart was still racing. I thought I'd conk out with the pill, but this was more than a panic attack. This was about Blake coming back into my life, warm eyed, firm bodied Blake.

I forced myself to get ready for bed. Brush teeth. Wash

face. brush hair. Check. Check that the lights were out in the other rooms and I'd set up the coffee for the morning. My favorite ratty nightgown was always a comfort, as was the stupid Cheshire Cat plush toy I cuddled when things got scary. Blake had given it to me.

The toy hit the door and slid to the floor. I plugged in my phone, made sure my cane was in reach and turned off the light, sliding under the comforter to try and sleep. After a minute I turned on the light again and picked up the toy. He slid under the comforter too.

7

BLAKE

I t had been easier at the restaurant. Joking around, playing with our food, chatting about our lives. At least until I saw the wince when her foot hit the floor and she picked up that damn cane.

My fucking fault.

When she invited me into her cottage, I thought I'd never stop smiling, but then I had to go and fuck everything up again with my call about Billy.

But dance was everything to her. Like me, she could pass on her passion to a whole new generation. She works with kids in her office. Why not with me?

I parked and walked to the red door. Freakin' Munchkin land cottage. She even had daisies in the garden. I knocked. No answer. I knocked louder. No luck.

Lights were out. I crept around back and tried to peer through a window I thought might be set into the wall of her bedroom. The room was dim, but she was sitting on the bed, a pillow on her lap.

An orange tabby jumped up on the inside sill and stared

at me through the window. He yowled and she jumped, wiping at her eyes.

Shit. She was crying.

She opened the window.

"You didn't even ask who's there. What if I was a burglar?"

"I know every one of your tricks." She wiped at her eyes with the back of her hand.

"Can I come in?"

"I guess." She pulled a tissue from a box near her bed, holding it crumpled in her hand.

"Are you going to open the front door?"

"No." Instead, she shoved the tissue into her pocket and jiggled the screen until it slid out of its slot.

"Oh. Okay."

After accidentally crushing a few flowers, I finagled my way through the window without much effort, hoping the people next door didn't keep a dog or security cameras. She'd set the screen on the floor by the wall, so I closed the window. "I think I might have killed a couple of your perky daisies. Hope Glinda doesn't come down hard on you."

"I hate those stupid flowers."

"Oh. Good." I slid my shoes off so I wouldn't track dirt in the bedroom. "Like old times, right?"

She smiled, and the expression warmed my heart. I didn't deserve her warmth. Hadn't earned it. But I soaked it up like a cat in a patch of sunlight.

"I remember. You used to climb the fire escape and sneak in through my window after midnight. Like Tony in West Side Story."

"You never turned me away." My body was tense with the need to pull her into my arms. To comfort her. The small blue trash can in the corner was piled high with crumpled tissues.

Her gaze was direct. Courageous. She'd been through hell and back. "You had a way of calming my nerves. Of making me see things in perspective. I've never laughed as much as I did when I was with you."

I stepped closer, lifting her hand and kissing her palm. "You still smell like honey."

"You picked the soap out at the store and gave it to me as an early Christmas present. I buy it for myself every December." I sat and she sniffed playfully at my neck. "You're wearing the same cologne."

"You told me you liked it."

"I did. I bet all your lovers like it." Anya winced. "Ugh. Sorry. That sounded snarky."

"Maybe I haven't worn it since the last time we were together." With a hand on her forearm, I tugged Anya closer, willing away the space between us. She didn't resist. Instead she flattened her hands and spread them out on my chest.

"You've filled out, Mr. Enfield."

I grinned. "I've been hitting the gym at the club. Do you remember the Gate Club?"

"So you're still a member of that cesspool of misogynism?"

"It's been a men's club since the 1800's. Tradition and all that."

The feel of her small hands sliding down my arms, pausing at the biceps. Squeezing. "Mmm. Nice. What time is it?"

"Around midnight."

"Not so late." She scooted closer, then stared at me for a full minute without talking. I was sure if I spoke, I'd kill the charged mood, so I kept my mouth shut and stared back, hoping this was leading where I desperately wanted it to lead. "Blake."

"Yeah?"

"Why did you come back?"

"I upset you. I wanted to apologize."

"I overreacted. I should have simply said thank you, but no. I hope you understand why I can't work in your studio."

"But..."

"Shush." She pushed the jacket off my shoulders and arms and let it fall to the floor.

"This may not be a great idea."

"I'm all cried out." Heat blazed in her eyes, the kind of heat that stirred my cock and tightened my balls. "I know you want me."

"I do, but..."

"Don't overthink this. It's sex. Nothing to do with love or commitment or any of that shit that doesn't apply to us. We're all grown up and we want each other. Why shouldn't we act on it?"

"No reason," I lied. Fucking Anya, then acting like nothing special had happened was going to rip open wounds.

"Take off your shirt."

I pulled the long sleeved tee over my head, tossing it on top of my jacket. She scanned my body, smiling at the noticeable bulge in my jeans.

"Pants." Her voice had dropped a tone. Sexy and needy. Anya directing the strip session was unbelievably hot, but it wouldn't last and she knew it.

"You're sure?"

"I told you..."

I picked her up, then laid her gently on the bed, the robe she was wearing opening at the bottom and showing off her pale, perfect legs. I straddled her thighs, plucking at the tie. "And what's under here?"

"More than you'll want to see. We can leave it on." She turned her head to the side.

"Anya..."

"It's not pretty."

"You'll always be beautiful to me."

"Blake. This is just sex. Don't try to make it more."

"Mmm hmm. Just sex." Only that would never be true for me. Not with this woman.

She bit her bottom lip and untied the belt, pulling the robe open and watching my face. My Anya was so strong. How could I not adore her?

Her skin was marked with lines of courage. Not scars. I leaned down and kissed the puckered lines on her hip, the thin stripe on her wrist, the larger reddened slash on her shoulder. Spreading her legs, I knelt between them, and kissing my way up her naked belly and chest, finally taking her mouth.

Anya had rarely wanted me gentle in bed, but in some ways this was a first time for us. From the moment I'd seen her across the street from my studio, I'd ached to hear her laugh, to see the heat in her eyes that hardened my cock, to spend a night inside her again.

"Tell me what you need, Empress."

"Give me everything."

8

ANYA

Blakes's laughter, strength, and spirit had supported me during my years as a dancer. In a tough, competitive world where eight ounces of weight gain, a rash of adolescent pimples or a day of cramps would keep you out of the running for a top level partner, Blake had chosen me. And stuck with me. And cared for me.

And lord, the sex. The intimacy and passion outside the studio had made us more than partners. More than lovers. At least until the end.

And in return, when I lay in the hospital, I'd refused to hear his explanation.

But tonight, as memories assaulted my mind and heart from every direction, I needed him again. Tomorrow I'd be back to myself. Focused on work and helping my clients. Tonight...

I gasped when he bit my shoulder. He was good at using his teeth. Just enough to drive me crazy.

"Where are you, Empress?"

"Here." I met his dark brown gaze and smiled.

"Take your own advice and stop thinking. We're here."

He licked one of my nipples and I arched into his wet mouth, clutching at his thick dark hair and pulling him closer.

"Again."

His smile was smug. "I want you so fucking bad." He ground against my sex, his jeans against my pussy.

"Take off the pants." I tugged at his waistband.

"When I'm ready."

Blake swiped two fingers back and forth over my wet nipple as he attacked the other one, licking then sucking until I moaned. "I need time to learn your body again. Do you still like this?"

He pinched my nipple, then twisted it. I arched, breathing faster. Heartbeat racing. My pussy throbbing. "Yes. Shit, yes."

"Are you wet for me?"

"I'm..." He twisted the second nipple and blood rushed to my sex, sensitizing every fold. "Oh, god. Again. I need it harder."

He moved lower. "Should I eat you up now? Or save you for dessert?"

Whimpering, I squirmed as he shifted to between my legs. My pussy clenched in anticipation. "Fuck me."

I'd lose my mind in his body like I used to, in the pleasure-pain, the musky scent and the rough fuck. He'd dominate, take everything until I was spent and sore and free in a way I'd never been with anyone else. Botched surgeries, upended dreams, impossible goals...forgotten with Blake's mouth on my body, his hands spreading my thighs, his cock pushing into my pussy.

"You smell so good." He worked two fingers inside my sex and grinned. "Tight. Soaked for me."

"I need you...inside." I thrust up to push him deeper.

"I'm inside you, Empress." As Blake lowered his face to my cunt he fucked me with his fingers, pressing exactly where I needed him to press, using his tongue over and over on my clit, each stroke timed to bring me to the edge. "Come for me. Right now."

I came hard, crying out. Twitching and throbbing and gasping, arching up to meet his thrusts. "Blake!"

He kept it up, watching my face with a shit eating grin. "When you come for me, you're even more beautiful."

"Take off your pants and fuck me."

"And you're still such a lady."

"Screw you."

"I might have to punish you for that."

"Try it."

"Stay there."

He popped into the bathroom and turned on the shower, then came as far as the doorway, completely naked. Blake was a very well formed male, taller than most dancers, with lean muscles that would make any woman take a second glance. His semi-hard cock hung large and thick.

He smiled mischievously and crooked a finger. "Let's play."

9

BLAKE

We slid into the shower and I immediately knelt at Anya's feet, carefully lifting her injured leg to rest on my shoulder.

"Wait. Don't you want…"

"I want more of this." She was open to me now. Open and completely vulnerable. I loved watching the water run over her beautiful pale skin, sometimes teasing her clit. But then the sprayer was my favorite shower toy. I licked her first, taking my time arousing her body. When she was ready I pushed two fingers inside her pussy, aiming the narrow spray of slightly warm water where it would make her come fast and hard.

Anya dug her nails into my scalp and shoulder, throwing back her head and closing her eyes. Her mouth grew slack as her body spasmed around my fingers. "Blake…"

I used my tongue as she came down from the intense orgasm, tasting her sweet, tart, musky flavor. Nothing at Bel Cielo's could ever match this.

We washed each other in a playful way, always exciting and erotic. She wanted to suck me off, but I slipped on a condom and lifted her, urging her legs around my waist. When I entered her tight sex, I moaned.

"God, Anya."

"Holy... I forgot... Oh... how big you are."

"You okay?"

"Give me a sec." She leaned in and kissed me, biting my lip almost hard enough to draw blood.

I didn't want rough. Rough was over too fast. I wanted to take her slow, to bring her toward pleasure with long strokes that filled her to the max then pressed against her sweet spot on the way out. I held her still against the wall.

"Anya..."

"Sex. Just sex."

To punctuate her statement, I yanked her firmly against my body.

"Oh! You bastard." But she wasn't really complaining.

I started to move, changing the angle when I knew she needed it. We'd been lovers for two years before the world came crashing down on both of us and had learned each other's preferences. Anya used sex as an escape, as a way to forget her financial and personal struggles. I'd been her first and only partner and she'd cared for me deeply. Sex for me had always been more about connection, not only exploring my partner's body, but learning what she held close to her heart. I'd hoped it was me she'd wrapped in the blanket of her love. But after the accident and her refusal to speak to me, I'd lost faith.

When Anya's breathing quickened, I plunged deeper, thrust faster. When she called out, I let myself go, her sex milking every drop of come from my throbbing cock. Spent and panting, I spread my fingers on the tile wall for support, my other hand cupping one of her butt cheeks.

She leaned her forehead against mine. "I'd forgotten how much I like playing with you."

I released my hold, allowing Anya to slide down my body, her expression sated and hazy, the looseness flowing down to her legs.

I lifted her rubbery body out of the shower and set her gently on the mat. We dried each other with care, taking turns to tease and scoot away. Only, instead of crawling into bed as was our past M.O., I dressed and kissed her. "I have another early day."

"You may as well stay up. It's three in the morning."

"If I stay until rush hour it will take too long to get back." I kissed her again. Couldn't resist. "I have time to take a nap after lunch."

"Hand me my robe, please."

She rose and saw me to the door, each step cooling our passion and putting more distance between us. "Come with me to Vic and Sloane's boat party next weekend. Lots of places to play on board. Vic and Dame will be happy to see you, and you'll love Sloane and Cassie."

I leaned in to kiss her again, but she scooted away. "Tonight was what I said. Just a night of sex and no more. If I go to the boat party, we aren't there as a couple. Just old friends. We won't be sharing a bed."

I ignored the comment. "One more kiss?"

Anya waved as I drove away, the hole in my heart I'd filled with our time together slowly draining. As a distraction, I queued up a favorites playlist and sang along with most of the songs on the drive back to the city.

I needed more time. More Anya. A chance to change her mine.

Hope was a determined bugger and it was already too late to shut the door in his face.

10

ANYA

The fog burned off quickly Friday morning, leaving the day a perfect blend of puffy clouds gliding across a bright blue sky. Blake picked me up early and drove us to his favorite breakfast joint near the marina.

"We're not due on the boat until ten." I said, sliding into the booth seat.

We ordered, drank coffee and chatted with the server until our food arrived.

I arched a brow at the huge helping of eggs, bacon, hash browns and toast on the plate in front of Blake. He grinned at my wary expression. "The sea air makes me hungry."

"You can eat all that?"

"Watch me."

"Where do you put it?"

"Dancing burns it up." He winced.

"I'm not made of crystal. You can mention dancing. You own a studio. I've seen you..."

He chewed and swallowed down a forkful of hash browns. They looked so delicious. "You've seen me dancing in the new studio?"

"Once or twice." More like five or six times. "I was walking by."

He scooped up another forkful of potatoes, then held it out for me. "You're not going to survive on that." He pointed to my fruit and yogurt.

"What if I get sea sick?"

"Then it won't matter what you have in your stomach. Might as well enjoy it."

"I've gone up a size."

He had the nerve to laugh. "What? From a zero to a two? You're more beautiful than ever." He glanced at my chest. "I especially like..."

"I know what you especially like."

"What do you think I especially like?"

I indicated my girls by spreading my hand across my chest. I was pretty proud of them too. As a teen, my flat chest had been a source of embarrassment, although never with Blake.

"Top three. Definitely."

"You have a top three?"

"What man doesn't have a top three?" he teased.

"Is this a generic top three or one based on my particular assets?"

"Your incredible assets are the only assets that interest me."

"Today."

He lowered his fork to the plate and wiped his mouth with his napkin. The warm gaze had darkened to a simmering heat. "I haven't been celibate, but I might bring something new to the mix you haven't thought about trying. We enjoyed experimenting, didn't we?"

I squirmed a little in my seat, his words sending heat spreading low in my belly. "We were crazy kids."

He smiled, slow and sensual. "When we're alone on the boat..."

"We won't be alone on the boat," I reminded him.

"Mmm hmm. Whatever you want, Empress."

I wanted Blake. Naked. Torturing him with my mouth or my hands the way he'd tortured me. He'd be up for the challenge, only... Blake wasn't on the menu. "I'd like a bite. A large one."

His eyes glittered with mischief, the skin around them crinkling. "I'm really hoping you're not referring to the hash browns."

I leaned forward and opened my mouth, moaning when the crispy, greasy, salty mound hit my tongue. I took my time chewing, telling myself this would be the only forbidden bite of the day. Blake's crooked smile and darkening eyes told me he wasn't thinking about hash browns either.

"Watching you eat is on my top three." He shifted position, wincing. "Don't suppose Vic would like it if we showed up late."

"Uncomfortable? Just so I'm clear, public restroom sex is also not happening."

"Today." His voice was a little hoarse. I rolled my eyes. "Don't knock it till you try it."

"I'll pass."

"Have you ever considered easing a man's discomfort in a restaurant booth?" He flashed his puppy dog eyes.

I laughed out loud, turning a few heads.

"Guess not, huh?" He sighed pitifully. "I'll eat my breakfast and think of something unpleasant. I should be able to walk in an hour or so."

I sucked on a strawberry and Blake cursed under his breath. For the first time in a long time I felt powerfully feminine. We'd had sex, but this was different. This was me showing him what he was missing.

Only I was an idiot. Getting us all worked up was the opposite of what I'd planned for the next two days. Too bad. I speared another forkful of hash browns. If I couldn't eat Blake, I'd settle for greasy breakfast food.

Forty-five minutes later we stood together on the long dock that led to Victor's catamaran, *Adagio*. Vic and Sloane were waiting at the far end of the ramp, ready to greet their visitors like royalty.

"Blake!"

We turned at the sound coming from behind us. A very tall man with dark hair and hazel green eyes smiled at Blake, then turned to me. "Anya? I'd heard a rumor but couldn't believe my ears."

"It's me. How are you Damien?"

"Better than I deserve, and all because of Cassandra." He tugged on the hand of a beautiful woman, dark haired and dark eyed, who stepped up beside him. She held out her free hand. "I'm Cassie."

"Anya. Great to meet you." Her eyes flitted to the cane, but she didn't comment on it. Someone else who probably knew at least part of the tale.

"Are you back in town permanently?" Damien asked.

"I have office hours two days a week near Blake's studio."

"Are you a doctor?" Cassie asked.

"A social worker."

"I'm trying to convince her to teach a couple of classes," Blake said.

"That would be great. He needs the help," Cassie said.

Damien laughed. "Luv, look at Vic's face." We all turned to see a handsome, but scowling man. "He's annoyed we've stopped in the middle of the dock and haven't proceeded in proper fashion toward our captain."

"You read each other's minds now, dear? You're definitely spending too much time together. Vic can wait." She turned back to me. "Have you met Sloane? She's amazing."

"I have. At her restaurant."

Blake tugged me forward. "Vic's anxious to see you again." We went on ahead as Cassie and Damien brought up the rear.

Vic grinned, surprising me with a huge hug. He, Blake and I had worked together often, picking out music for our routines. "It's so good to see you, Yaya."

"I forgot you used to call me that."

"I suits you."

"Not anymore."

"Anya it is. You look great. But what are you doing with this loser?"

"I've been asking myself the same question, although he did give me half his hash browns."

"Hey! I'm irresistible." Blake tugged me away from Vic and draped a long arm over my shoulder.

I ducked away. "Irrepressible maybe," I said.

"Irredeemable," Sloane said, smiling a welcome at me and ignoring Blake.

"Irrefutable!" Blake was getting into this.

"Irremovable." Vic gave Blake a push toward the gangplank.

"Okay, okay. I'm going. Jeez." He took away my cane and offered me his arm. The puppy dog pleading look, an expression I'd never been able to ignore, worked. For some reason having me here on this outing with his friends was important to Blake. I made a note to ask him about it later.

"Rach and Marley had to bow out. One of the twins has

the sniffles." Damien said as we walked past the galley and into the surprisingly large living room style cabin. Comfy looking couches and chairs, small tables attached to the walls and floors so they wouldn't go flying around in rough weather and a small bar in the corner made up the interior. Everything was decorated in shades of cream and tan with brighter accents added by curtains, pillows and even fresh flowers. It was lovely and homey. Not at all ostentatious.

"That'll be you next year." Blake said, looking at Cassie.

"The doctor has assured us Cassandra is carrying one perfect child. Quite enough," Damien announced in his slightly British accent, as if he had any say.

I glanced at Cassie and smiled. Her baby bump was just showing. "Congratulations," I said.

"Thank you." She beamed at Damien who'd taken on that smug expression men get when they think they'd accomplished something amazing. I held back the eye roll. To his credit he tugged Cassie closer and kissed her cheek, whispering something that made her smile and even blush.

Okay, they were kind of adorable, and I never in a million years would have thought of Damien Granger as adorable. Hot, yeah, if you liked Alpha males with a capital A. Formidable, definitely. Sometimes even scary. Damien and Victor had been involved in some pretty rough stuff during their high school and college days, but for some reason they'd accepted Blake and Marley into their small social circle and protected the dancer and the nerd from the bullies who ran rampant in the high cost private school they'd attended. Even so, I'd always felt more comfortable with Vic, since he'd written and produced most of our dance music in his recording studio, then come by to cheer us on in local competitions.

Busily chomping on an appetizer, Victor wore a black

tee shirt and black jeans, the tats at the bottom of his neck peeking out when he moved. His new wife, Sloane, wore a "Save the Mission" tee shirt, ripped up designer jeans and rubber soled slip on shoes designed for boating. Cassie was in a brightly colored silk blouse, navy capris and sandals. Her toe nails were red, white and blue. I stared down at my choice of attire.

Plain jeans and sneakers, my favorite pink pullover sweater and a baseball cap for a team that bombed this year. I didn't spend much on clothes as most of my money went toward rent, but my practice was doing well and I had nothing to be ashamed of.

Blake held out a plate stacked with appetizers. "Eat."

"We just had breakfast."

"Eat or Drew will raise a ruckus."

"Drew?"

"Hello, Blake." A slim man with thinning blonde hair and a bit of ginger stubble turned to smile at me. His apron said, "Hot and Spicy (and the food's good too) "Hello, I'm Drew, and despite the *lawyer's* arguments to the contrary, I have never raised a ruckus."

Victor coughed in a meaningful way.

"Well, not recently."

"Hi, Drew. I'm Anya."

"*The* Anya? The girl he..." Drew winced a moment later, realizing he might have made a mistake letting on he knew my backstory.

The cabin grew silent. I took in a deep breath and stared the others down. "If anyone shows me one iota of pity, I'll bop you on the head with my cane and toss you overboard. It's been more than ten years and I'm fine."

Damien broke the silence with a hearty laugh. Sloane

clapped her hands. "You and I are going to be best friends. I know it."

Drew took my hand. "I'm so sorry. I shouldn't have said it that way. It's very nice to meet you, Anya."

"Are you the galley slave?" I teased.

"Yes, but I don't mind. My partner Paul and I run an antique shop in the Castro District and it's so nice to get out on the water once in a while. It's like a paid vacation."

"I'm guessing Paul's the captain?"

"First mate. Vic insists on being called Captain. Of course, he was raised around boats and has taken all the certifications. He's earned the title of captain. Almost."

I laughed as Vic pretended to snarl. "Don't listen to the scurvy crew. I've had to keel haul them several times this summer for mouthing off." Drew shook his head and returned to the galley. Vic tapped Blake on the shoulder. "Any message from Val?"

"You know Val. Always late."

"Your sister's coming?" I whispered.

He led me away from the others. "Yep. With her nurse."

"Is she ill?"

"She was in an accident."

"Oh, I'm sorry."

"C'mon. Let's take a look at the bay." He took my hand, led me to a cushioned bench and pulled me down next to him.

The view of the Golden Gate Bridge was amazing, with the bay to the right and the Pacific to the left, it stood as a sentinel to guide drivers and boaters to the beautiful San Francisco Bay Area. The bridge was magnificent today with the bright blue California sky and the hills of Marin County as background. Made me wish I'd brought my camera. I was just thinking about going back inside to get my phone so I could take a picture when Blake leaned over and whispered.

Which cabin did Vic give you?"

"He hasn't said, but it doesn't matter. I'm sleeping alone on this trip. I'm serious."

He laughed. "You just about blew my socks off the other night." He glanced down at his feet. "Look. I'm still feeling the aftereffects."

I couldn't hold back the smile. He was wearing sandals. "I'm serious."

"But..."

I paced to the railing, not wanting to see his face change, to hear him tell me he wouldn't go along with what I was suggesting. "I've thought about this for the last few days. Hear me out."

"Anya." His hands slid along my shoulders from behind, snaking down my arms to twine his fingers with mine. Possessive, yet tender. Perfect. "I'm listening."

I forced myself to stand still, to resist leaning back. I ached for him. I'd always ached for him.

I was too old to play games. I'd be truthful. "As much as my body is onboard with taking you to bed, my heart is set on something more."

"I don't..."

"It's okay. I'm not asking for a proposal. We hardly know each other, and that's the problem. Our night together was so good. That aspect of our relationship has always been great. But what I felt for you when I was twenty probably wouldn't have lasted. I wanted a career most of all, a life in the spotlight. At that time I would have worked toward that end even if it meant splitting up. You were the love of a twenty year old woman's life. I'm not that person anymore. You're not that twenty one year old guy anymore either."

"I was an idiot back then. A kid who didn't know how good he had it." He released one of my hands and nudged a clump of hair out of the way, leaving my ear exposed.

"I want to find out who you are now. Who we are together. Without dance as our anchor."

"Dance is still a part of my world. You know that."

"I'm okay with you running a studio. I'm talking about us." I found the courage to turn in his arms and take a step back. He let me go, giving me his complete attention. "When we were dancing, every minute of our lives was scheduled. Sex was our outlet. We skipped over the way real couples get together, sharing their time in a less structured way.

"You want to start fresh? Maybe date?"

"Yes. That's exactly what I want."

"And no sex?"

"Does it matter?"

"I want you. All the time. You keep me up at night. So yes, it matters. But I want you to be comfortable with us even more. To trust me. To believe like I do that we belong together."

"Do you believe that?"

"Anya..." He rested his forehead on mine. "There's no one else for me. You're the one."

"But how much do you know about who I am now?"

"Not as much as I'd like to know." His warm breath tickled my ear. "Dating is great. I can't wait to take you to my favorite restaurants, to clubs, movies, whatever you want. But kissing is great too. He bit my earlobe and I gasped. "And nibbling. I like nibbling." He licked the spot below the lobe. "Hearing you make those sexy noises when I worship your pussy."

"You're impossible."

"C'mon. You love it."

"I can resist your charms."

"You think so now."

I squeezed my legs together. This was going to be harder than I thought.

"Empress, I'll go on dozens of dates if that's what you want, but I get hard when I'm in the same room with you. So, yeah. I'll be subtle about it, but I'm going to do my best. And you only have to say no once. Deal?"

I was going to regret this, but I could handle Blake. "Deal."

"Excellent." He surprised me with a playful, sweet as sugar kiss. "Just to seal the deal."

"Val's here!" Vic shouted.

Val arrived in an electric wheelchair, followed by a guy who could be a GQ model. "That's her nurse?"

"We call him that. His name is Gordon. They've been dating for two years. He's besotted, but she's not ready to commit. At least that's what she tells me." Blake frowned. "I think the guy's after her money. I'm thinking of talking to Dame and Vic about it."

"Whoa. You're acting like an uber overprotective big brother. I get it. But give the guy a chance."

"I can never talk to her alone. He's always there."

"How about if Cassie and Sloane invite her for a girls night out?"

Blake turned to stare at me. "One more reason to love you."

"Don't say that."

"Why?"

"You're not serious and I don't think love is something to joke about."

"What if I told you I was being serious?"

"Blake." I touched his face and he automatically turned into my palm. "Slow, remember. One step at a time."

He lowered his voice and used a Cuban accent like his mom's. "Slow steps can be muy sexy."

I made a show of shaking my head, really wanting to laugh. He could make me smile faster than anyone I knew.

Gordon carried Val inside, setting her onto the couch as Damien brought up the folded wheelchair. She was a beauty, with the same full, dark head of hair and large brown eyes as her brother, although her face was more almond than square and her cheek bones more pronounced. Her light brown skin spoke of their lovely Cuban/African ancestral mix, and the smile she gave her brother was as bright as the California sky.

Blake kissed his sister's forehead then plunked down on the couch beside her, making Gordon scowl. He'd definitely had his eye on that seat. "Hey squirt. You're the best kind of surprise."

Hi Blake." She gave her brother a peck on the cheek then slid her gaze from Blake to me. She smiled and extended her hand, hesitating at the last minute. "Anya?"

"Hi Val."

"I...I didn't know you were back in town." She punched Blake on the arm. "Dope! Why didn't you tell me you two were back together? This is great news."

"Oh...we're not. Not in that way. I share an office with another colleague near Blake's studio. We ran into each other a couple of weeks ago." I didn't mention how I'd practically stalked him.

"Aw." She shrugged. "Too bad. He's been carrying a torch for you since...you know."

Val pointed at her legs, which confused the hell out of me. What did our splitting up have to do with her accident?"

I leaned a little closer, softening my voice. "If you don't mind my asking, when..."

Blake jumped up. "We're casting off now, right Vic? We're already an hour past schedule."

Vic narrowed his eyes, twisting his mouth into a frown and aiming it at Blake. "Yeaaah." He put down his beer and straightened up. "All experienced hands on deck. Dame and Blake on the dock. Cassie to the bow, Sloane the stern. Hold off and wait for my signal. A wind's picked up and Paul and I will need to check the readings."

"Aye, Captain."

Gordon poured a glass of white wine and brought it to Val. She shook her head and he offered it to me.

"Thank you."

"Would you like water or a soda?" he asked Val.

"Sparkling water. Thanks. Give me a few, okay?"

"Let me know if you need anything. I'm gonna watch the show."

"We landlubbers have to stay inside the cabins unless we want to get knocked over by the crew." Val said. "Or worse."

"I'm fine right here." I was surprised by how quickly the group spilt up and headed to what must be their assigned areas. Damien stood by the forward starboard line, watching for Victor's signal.

Vic hopped down the last few steps and caught Dame and Blake's gaze. "We'll be springing off the dock. Wind's coming from the north. You know the procedure. Dame?"

"Aye, Captain."

"Blake?"

"Aye, sir."

"We have the hottest crew of pirates ever seen in the bay," Val giggled.

"Do you want to get closer to the window?"

She glanced at Gordon. "I'm fine."

"I'm stronger than I look. I can bring your limo around and get you over to the window in no time." I tilted my head toward the folded up wheelchair.

"No really. It's fine. I'm happy chatting with you."

Victor quick stepped over the deck to the bow, releasing a cylindrical cushion along the starboard side. "Dame, untie the line and toss it to Cassie. Then set this spring line to that cleat near the stern." Vic tossed Damien another line. "Just a loop no knot. Blake, untie the stern line and toss it to Sloane, then hop back on. Be aware, we'll be backing out. Dame, when you're done, hop on and stand by to release the spring line."

"Aye."

Vic signaled to Paul. "Port engine. Slow ahead."

The rear end of the boat began to drift out. Vic watched its movement like a hawk watched its prey, all the while judging angles and windspeed.

"Wind's steady, Captain." Paul shouted.

"Dame, release the line. Paul, both engines slow reverse."

"Clear off the dock, Captain."

"Ahead at your discretion, Number Two."

Before we knew it we were in clear water, moving toward the Golden Gate and lands beyond.

My heart pounded with the excitement of leaving civilization behind and journeying somewhere new. Maybe all the silly seafaring talk had struck a chord

"You okay, Empress?"

"You looked like you knew what you were doing."

"Hey, despite what Sloane says, I'm a regular on this piece of driftwood."

Vic came over, taking me aside. "Would you like to see

the rest of *Adagio*?"

"I'd love to." Vic led me out to the aft deck, which had a removable canvas roof for shade but plenty of sun as well. Lounge chairs and small fold out tables were set up for those who wanted to catch some rays. Gordon had already claimed a spot.

The bridge was behind us now. We turned north, heading to a national park Blake and I had visited years ago on one of our rare days off. Victor had plans anchor Adagio in the inlet for two nights so we could take day trips to check out the quaint town. Damien and Cassie had decided to spend their two nights at a swanky hotel, Damien feeling his pregnant wife needed a proper bed.

"Are you in the same business as Damien?" I asked Cassie.

"I'm an artist and I own the art studio and gallery across the street from Sloane's restaurant. I've also worked a lot of art restoration jobs. I can't do it now, because of the chemicals."

"That's wonderful. I'd love to see your work. I have no artistic talent at all. I mean…you know what I mean."

"Victor told me, when you and Blake danced together he forgot to breathe."

"He must have been teasing you."

"How many competitions did you win?"

"Only national ones. For our age groups."

"Only?"

"Sydney was going to be a life changer, as it happened, my life changed anyway. I'm happy with the choices I've made. I love my work."

"C'mon, I'll show you around downstairs." Vic offered me his arm and shook his head at Blake, who was about to follow. "This is the Port pontoon, the Guest Galley I call it."

Dame and Cassie would normally stay here in the largest room, but since they're staying on shore, I'm giving it to Val and Gordon. There's more room for her wheelchair if she needs it. We have an elevator on this side."

"Really? An elevator?"

"It's come in handy since she's agreed to come on trips with us. Socializing has made a huge difference. She's a terrific woman. So strong. I'm proud she considers Sloane and me friends."

"She's grown into a beautiful young woman, but what's with Gordon?"

"Don't get me started. She doesn't want to live at home. She'd prefer to be independent, but she's lonely too. She was always a social kid."

He opened a door half way down the corridor.

"This is your room. You did want your own room, right?"

"Yes, definitely." I looked around. A double bed. A comfy looking chair. "This is great."

"You have to share the head with Blake. And the shower. Sorry."

"That's fine. Where's Blake going to sleep?"

"In the main cabin. The couches turn into beds. Or he can take the kid's room if he prefers. It's in the bow right next door."

I laughed. "Is the bed large enough?"

"Standard twin."

"He can have my room."

"No. You're my special guest. Blake's like a little brother. He gets whatever's left."

I sat on the edge of my bed. "So you, Sloane, Cassie and Blake all work on the same block?"

"I have a recording studio not too far away, but Dame

and I bought the building Blake's studio and Sloane's restaurant is in. Have you seen the dance studio?"

"Only from the outside."

"It's designed to be practical and elegant. I was shocked when I saw it."

"Blake has a good eye."

"The work he does with his students and the music industry professionals is amazing. You should make him show you around."

I sighed and glanced away. "He wants me to teach a couple of classes." I glanced down at my leg. "I don't see how..."

"Did your teachers do all the steps with you when they taught class?"

"No. Of course not."

"Give it a try. I don't remember the last time I saw Blake this happy."

I frowned. "Look, I know he's your friend but..."

"I'm being an ass. I'm sorry. I have no right to even suggest you...I don't know...forgive him? He was going through hell at the time. Yeah, he should have called off the rehearsal, but his sister was in a coma. He'd been..."

"What?"

We stared at each other for a full minute. "He didn't tell you."

"That his sister had been seriously hurt? Back when... No. What the fuck happened?" I stood, taking a step toward Vic.

"The night before your last rehearsal, Val took Blake's Porsche without permission to go to a party. A drunk driver forced her off the road. Two of her friends were in the car with her. They walked away with only a few scratches. No drugs or alcohol in their systems so the blame was laid on the drunk asshole who's still rotting in prison for what he did. But that doesn't give Val back what she lost."

"And Blake..."

"He left the keys where she could grab them. Blake blamed himself."

"Of course he did." I lowered my body to the bed. "Holy shit. Why didn't he tell me?"

"You didn't talk to him either. About the rumor you heard."

"Olav sent me pictures. It wasn't a rumor."

"Dame and I tracked the asshole down. Olav came clean."

"What?"

"He confessed to lying about the whole thing, but Blake wouldn't let us contact you. He said you needed time to heal." Vic had always been the protective type. Even though he was angry with me, I loved the way he stood up for his longtime friend. "You and Blake danced together for how many years?"

"Almost twelve."

"And how long did you know Olav?"

"He and Shannon and Blake and I had competed against each other for five years or so."

"But you believed him over Blake. You refused to speak to your own partner."

"All I could think about was how my lifelong dream had been crushed by a guy I thought I could trust with my life." I stood, shaking my head, clutching at the hem of my sweater. "I'd been so frantic about the competition. We'd stopped communicating completely during the month we'd stayed apart. There was one section giving us trouble and I thought it would help us focus if we weren't...spending nights together." I limped to the tiny window, needing some air.

Vic opened it for me. "Never works. Just drives you crazy."

I leaned my forehead against the cool sill. "What now?" The scent of the sea always calmed me, but tonight it was a pale substitute.

"At the risk of getting slapped or whacked with that lethal cane of yours, it's not too late."

"You're safe. I left the cane upstairs." I squeezed his arm. "You've always been a dreamer, Vic. A romantic. But I like you anyway."

"I know." He grinned. "You two make sense, the way Sloane and I do. Give him a chance."

"Maybe I'm not worth the chance."

Vic laughed. "You walk on water as far as Blake is concerned."

"He doesn't know me anymore."

"That kind of shit is easy to fix."

Vic helped me back up the stairs and I parked in an outdoor lounge chair set in a shady spot. Borrowing sun screen from Sloane despite the awning, I asked Drew for some fizzy water with lemon and relaxed back into the seat. Someone started up a mellow playlist.

Blake had carried Val from the main cabin and helped her into her motorized chair. She parked it near Gordon and he pulled her into his lap, whispering something that made her laugh. Maybe he wasn't such a tool after all.

Or maybe I was being the dreamer.

I closed my eyes and must have drifted off, because when I opened them, Blake was in the chair next to mine, his body twisted to face me, his expression wary. The afternoon had gotten cooler and someone had tucked a blanket around me.

"Hi," he said, the corners of his mouth curling softly.

I smiled, wondering how anyone could ever resist the magic of his soulful eyes. "Did your front man give a full report?"

"Front man?"

"Don't play innocent. Did you ask Vic to get me alone in order to enlighten me about what really happened on that night?"

"No. I was furious. Still am. I wanted to talk to you about everything, but I didn't know how to broach the subject. I thought maybe tonight, when we were alone..."

"What did I tell you?"

"We wouldn't be alone on the boat, yet here we are."

Everyone else was in the main cabin or on the front deck. I glanced down. He'd pushed his lounge chair up against mine as I'd slept, not an inch of space between them. "Victor wasn't gentle with his delivery. Give me a chance to digest the information."

"Why, so you can come up with another reason why we shouldn't be together?"

Spot on. Blake knew me too well. "When you say *together* you mean something other than what we shared at my home."

"Yes, only your heart isn't open to that possibility, is it? You've walled it up securely, haven't you? Life is safe and predictable. And lonely."

"I suggested dating."

"And I told you that would be awesome, but you need me for more than an escort around town. Why did you keep coming around to watch me? Why are you afraid to admit you're happy when we're together?"

Blake snaked his hand under the blanket, grasping my hand and lifting to his mouth. His was cold and large and I shivered remembering how his fingers had felt inside my pussy.

"I'm not afraid."

He kissed each finger. "I want you. Every bit of you. Your nose when it wrinkles and your smile when it spreads across your face and lights up my world. Your eyes when they fill with passion or tears. Your scars, inside and out. Your sadness. Your laughter. Your courage. You, Anya. I want you."

Blake's kiss wasn't gentle. His tongue met mine with fierceness, his lips almost bruising as he forced my head back into the hand he rested at my nape. I clutched at his shoulders, his hair, giving back in full measure the passion he was sharing with me.

The wall around my lonely heart began to crumble, but I wasn't ready. I closed off all emotion other than lust and brought his hand to my ass.

"Mmm." He squeezed my cheek. "Perfect." He'd lowered the tone of his voice, whispering his comment so close to my ear the warmth of his breath stirred the random threads of my hair

"I want to bite it. Hard."

"You do?"

"Mmm. Both cheeks. Maybe spank them."

"Spank them?" I squirmed on the chair, pressing my legs together.

He chuckled softly. "You used to like that. I'd kiss and lick those perfect cheeks, spread your legs and use my fingers inside your wet pussy. You used to like all our games."

I closed my eyes and swallowed hard. "Sex has never been our problem."

"And that's just it. We didn't have a problem until I

fucked up. So here's the question. You know the truth now. Can you let me love you the way I've wanted to love you since the first day you admitted feeling the same way about me?"

"I was seventeen." The sound of music broke into my lust filled hazy brain. "Is that Victor playing?"

"He's trying out a new song."

All his sexy talk had made me achy. I needed a distraction.

"Why don't we go in and listen?" I glanced around. "No one else is out here."

"I know." Under the blanket Blake stroked my thigh, moving his hand toward the inside, using his knuckles to trace a line straight to my core.

My breaths came in short gasps, stopping completely when he found my clit with his knuckle. He rubbed, using a rhythm that had be arching up.

"Shhh." He leaned close enough to kiss me, but his next words made me tremble. "Touch your nipples." He'd always loved to watch me bring myself close to peaking.

"Blake."

"You're going to come. Right here. With everyone else in the next room."

My blood had deserted my brain, making a beeline to my sex. "Blake..."

"Say yes. I want to bring you pleasure."

"What happened...happened to slow?"

"Did I jump you?" He kissed my throat.

I laughed softly. Couldn't help it. Victor was singing one of his first romantic hits now, putting a different spin on the melody.

Blake moved his hand to my waist, letting it rest there until I gave him permission. His pinky slid under my waistband. My lower belly twitched in anticipation as his eyes gleamed with lust.

"Yes."

His smile spoke of a hundred wicked things as he unbuttoned and unzipped my fly. "I'm going to play with your pussy. No one will know, but you'll have to stay very still. Close your eyes." With some maneuvering Blake slid my jeans down to my ankles, but not off. Imagine your ankles are tied and your knees are forced apart. Can't move your legs unless I tell you to. Have to take what I give you without moving an inch. Say yes."

"Yes."

This was going to be torture. Exactly what he loved to do. What I loved too.

Blake was reawakening my wild side only that wasn't me anymore. Unless maybe it was. I'd been holding it at bay. Waiting for...

One finger swiped across my clit. "Oh god."

"Shhh. No words. Only sweet sexy noises."

He bit my lip then licked it, unfastening the front of my bra, then bringing one of my hands up, using my fingers to stroke my own nipple. "You can move this hand. I'll tell you when to stroke. When to pinch. When to twist."

"Bossy."

He pinched my clit and I jumped. "No more warnings." Spreading my knees was easier now that he'd pulled down my jeans. "You're so fucking wet for me. I want to taste you. Maybe later."

He fucked me with his large fingers, starting with two, then three, using his thumb on my clit. When I spoke a word, he pulled his hand away, but when I moaned or whimpered he rewarded me with harder strokes.

I bit my arm to muffle my cry when I came, the orgasm

sending waves of ecstasy through every cell, my pussy throbbing so violently I thought Blake's fingers might bruise. Blake and I had always toyed with the exciting idea of fucking with strangers nearby, the danger of discovery a terrific turn on.

"I wish we could fuck under the stars tonight." He licked one of his previously occupied fingers. "As delicious as I'd hoped."

Still high from the experience, I grabbed his hand and sucked on another. "Needs salt."

He had to bury his face in the blanket to keep from laughing out loud.

I picked up my cane and took the port side staircase to my room to clean myself up, changing my panties in the process. They were soaked and smelled strongly of my arousal, so I washed them out and draped them on the wooden chair back. Someone in the other room must have known what we were doing, but I couldn't dredge up the energy to care. Blake was bringing me back to life, and my body was glorying in each rough and gentle touch, each sweet or ravaging kiss. Each teasing order and satisfied grin.

A twinge of guilt broke into my happy mood. He'd admitted this meant more to him that physical release. The last thing in the world I wanted to do was hurt him, but could I ever make a man as loving and generous as Blake happy? He said he wanted me. Me. Not some fantasy of me. I sighed the headed back for the stairs.

Sloane and Drew had taken over in the galley, dishing out what looked like a delicious meal. The main course was pecan crusted salmon, mini garlic potatoes and avocado caprese salad. Delicious rolls that Sloane had baked at home and reheated on board accompanied the feast along with olive oil for dipping and also a lovely herb butter spread.

Needless to say, everyone enjoyed the meal immensely.

Near the end of dinner, Cassie told Victor she wanted to dance with her baby daddy. Damien was very close to rolling his eyes, but when Vic began to play the song Cassie had requested, he acquiesced with a wide grin. In fact I'd never seen Damien smile as much as he had today. They made a beautiful couple.

Gordon surprised everyone by lifting Val and dancing with her in his arms. She beamed, beautiful and happy.

Sloane looked to Blake, then me, then Blake. "C'mon you two."

Ice traveled down my spine from my nape to my lowest vertebrae. Blake took my hand and led me to the bar. "I think maybe just a drink tonight. Hm?"

He'd tried to save me from humiliation with a simple gesture, but it was too late. I couldn't dance. My third surgery can gone horribly wrong and my right leg was a little shorter than my left. I'd never find my center. Never turn or move with grace again. Never dance.

I froze in place, watching Cassie and Damien slow and look in our direction. Vic stopped playing.

"I'm sorry. I think I'll...I'll..." I backed away several steps, reaching for my cane which I'd left leaning against the wall.

"There might be shooting stars tonight. Let's check." Blake took my hand and led me to the bow deck, rescuing me from startled looks and embarrassed glances. We found a seat on the bench we'd used before.

Sloane showed up a minute later. "I'm so sorry. I'm a world class idiot."

"It's okay. I overreacted."

"No it isn't. I work in a kitchen with a staff who have

no filters, who talk about everyone's business. I'm not great in classy social situations. I have no filters and talk before I think things through. I should have realized if you'd wanted to dance, you would have been dancing already."

The music had stopped. "I think I ruined everyone's evening."

"No. No, you didn't. Come back inside. It's damp and foggy."

I looked to Blake. "I'll brave the fog if you want to stay," he said.

"We'll go back. I'll explain."

"You don't have to..."

"I do. I think for me more than anyone."

People were chatting softly. Everyone smiled when I came back in. "Vic, can you start up the music?"

He did, smiling and winking at me, offering me support in a very Victorish way.

Blake was at my back. His large hand on my waist.

"I haven't danced since the accident. When you've trained your whole life to do something and you can't do it the way you were trained, it hurts to even think about trying. At least it has up until now."

Damien asked Sloan for a dance, since she hadn't had a chance with Vic playing. When they finished, Gordon, who'd danced every dance with Val, put her down on a chair, kissed her cheek and asked Vic if he could use Vic's acoustic guitar to play a song. Vic agreed, anxious to wrap his arms around his beautiful wife.

I didn't know the guy at all but everyone else looked pretty shocked when Gordon played a cool version of *Kiss Me*, singing in a clear, husky voice. Val's smile was angelic, pride written in the glitter of her eyes.

When Vic packed up his guitar, everyone chatted over desserts that included fruit tarts and chocolate brownies.

"You have a great voice. And you play well." I told Gordon.

"Thank you," Gordon smiled, transforming his wary expression into a much more relaxed one. He was a beautiful man in a room with several other males cut from the same cloth, at least on the surface. Gordon closed off his emotions from everyone but Val, whether it was self-protection, indifference or surrender, I couldn't say.

"You have an office near Vic's studio? What kind of business?"

"I'm a social worker. A lot of my clients are kids working through trauma."

"You sound like you like your work."

"I love it."

I glanced at Val. "Are you a nurse?"

"I'm an EMT, but Val's family hires me in for situations like this where she has to travel and can't always use the chair. Vic, Damien and Blake call me her nursemaid as a joke. They never say it in front of Val."

"I've noticed some tension in the room."

"I'm here 'cause Val likes to spend time with her brother and her friends. I don't really care what they think. Sloane and Cassie are okay with me." He shrugged.

"You've been wonderfully attentive. She seems to adore you."

He grinned. "I love Val. It started out as a job, but... everything changed as soon as I got to know her. I try not to hover. Val wants to be independent. Sometimes I need time too."

"Of course you do. People often see only the stress of the victim and not the caregivers."

"You must have a ton of clients."

"I have just the right amount."

As couples headed off to bed, I poured myself another glass of wine and relaxed into one of the comfy chairs in the main cabin. I knew if I tried to sleep I'd toss and turn and end up exhausted in the morning. My brain had too many things to sort through before it would clear and allow me to rest.

Blake knelt in front of my chair, rubbing his hands up my thighs. I covered them with mine. "I'd like to be alone for a while," I said, trying not to look at his beautiful eyes.

"You're in my bedroom."

"Oh, shit, I forgot." I started to stand but he pressed me down. "I can sit outside," I protested. "Or in the galley."

"I want you here."

"Blake..."

"Stay with me tonight. Let me hold you. Just that."

"It's never just that."

His impish smile sent shivers to all the wrong places. Or maybe the right places. "I might play with your hair, or nibble your ear, but I'll behave, I promise."

"I don't think I can behave if we're that close." No reason to lie.

"I think we can. I have faith in us. You used to have faith in us too."

"You mean, I used to have faith in you."

He turned away and walked to a cabinet, pulling out sheets, pillows and blankets.

"Blake..."

"Leave if you want. Or stay."

He didn't offer to help me down the stairs to my cabin or up the stairs to the galley. What had he expected? That when I found out the truth about that night I'd jump into his arms and beg him to forgive me? That I'd... I'd admit how much I wanted him, needed him. Even loved him, and that it was anger holding me back? Or fear? Or fucking stubborn pride?

I could have tried to dance with him. No one here would have looked at me with pity. My face heated with shame. I should buy the tee shirt. *Too Gutless to Try.*

Wrapping my arms around my body, I sat on the second step leading up to the galley. At least he couldn't say I was in his bedroom. I folded my arms on bent knees and rested my cheek in the nest. The stars and moon were invisible tonight, the fog shroud covering everything that might have distracted me. Instead I closed my eyes and concentrated on the sounds Blake made as he pulled out the couch, tucked in sheets and arranged the blanket.

I opened my eyes when he kicked off his shoes and pulled off his socks and shirt. He met my gaze as he unzipped his jeans, tossing them onto the same pile he'd made in a nearby chair, leaving on his boxer briefs for the sake of propriety. Blake was glorious dressed or undressed, but almost-naked Blake was the most enticing.

Ignoring me, he walked to the bar, filling a glass of water and downing it in three gulps. He brushed his teeth in the bar sink, turned off the lights and walked back to the makeshift bed.

Yeah, I'd hurt him and he was pissed. Time to pull my head out of my ass and fix this.

"If you need help with anything, Paul and Drew are still up. Goodnight, Anya." He slid under the covers, turned his back and closed his eyes.

I didn't move. Tonight wasn't ending like this. After about five minutes he turned around. "Your glaring is drilling a hole in my back."

"I'm mining for your heart."

"Aiming to do more damage?"

"Hoping the opposite. Can we talk?"

He sighed and lay on his back, staring at the ceiling. "I'm tired, Empress."

At least he was calling me Empress again. "I'm sorry if I hurt you."

He closed his eyes, taking in a deep breath and blowing it out through pouted lips. "One of these days I'm gonna end up in the looney bin because of you."

"I don't mean to be difficult."

"My offer still stands." He pushed aside the covers and arched an eyebrow.

"Cuddling?"

"Cuddling."

I stripped off my sweater, sneakers and jeans, leaving on my socks, bra and panties and sliding in next to him. He was warm and large and his scent reminded me of how I used to feel safe when we were together. Like nothing could touch me, I turned to shift into the usual spoon position, my back to his front, but he stopped me with a hand on my hip. "I'd rather see your face when we talk."

"You still want to talk?" I asked while I twisted around.

"I want to know why."

"Why?"

"Why you still can't trust me. If you ever will."

His jaw was tense, his frown making my chest ache. I'd brought this on. Hesitating I smoothed the lines between his large dark eyes with my thumb. He didn't push me away. When I pressed my palm against the stubble on his cheek, he tilted his face against my hand. I smiled, meeting his gaze. "I trust you with my life."

"And with your heart?"

My chest twinged, the pain in his eyes bringing tears to mine. "Yes. With my heart too."

"I want to believe that."

"I haven't been open with you. I'm sorry. I urge my clients to be honest and move forward. But I'm the worst of the lot."

"You have to know I'd never hurt you."

"I do, I do." I blew out a breath. "Imagine if we'd both been honest about what was going on in our heads the morning of our rehearsal." I held up my hand when he started to protest. "Okay. Yeah, we might have argued and stormed off, but I could have been there with you during Val's ordeal. I wish I'd been brave enough to bring up what I'd heard about you and Shannon. I wish I'd been brave enough to dance with you tonight."

"I've never stormed off."

"Yeah, that would have been me," I admitted. "But I'm not that hot headed dancer anymore."

He stroked my hair. My face. "What is it you want from me, beautiful woman?"

I started to say friendship, but no. I wanted a lot more than that. "I want you to be the Blake you've always been. Affectionate. Protective. A sex god." He laughed. "A man with a heart large enough to care for me, despite my craziness."

"To care for you?

"That's what I want."

"And what about you? Will you...care for me back?"

"I do. You mean a lot to me."

"Mmm hmm."

I wasn't saying what he wanted to hear, but I couldn't. Not yet. "Hanging with me is probably going to involve a lot of patience on your part."

"I'm not arguing with that assessment. What about the teaching job at my studio?"

"Blake!" I didn't hide my irritation.

"Too soon? Huge mistake to bring it up or forgivable misstep?"

"Please. Teaching would just be...it would hurt, you know?"

"I get why you feel this way, but can I be honest?"

"Sure."

"If you don't try, you'll never know. Come to the recital next weekend. See the kids. Val will be there. She's one of my chief assistants."

"I've heard great things about what you've accomplished. Videos and tours? Amazing."

"Vic got me my first big name client, then I found out word of mouth was as powerful as social media, at least at that level."

I leaned closer and gave him a swift kiss. "You deserve every bit of your success. I'm proud to say I was there for the very first number you choreographed."

"Uh huh. Wasn't that a Justin Timberlake song you played ad nauseam?" Blake traced my cheekbone with a calloused finger. His breath smelled of mint, his body of his own uniquely delicious scent.

"Mmm hmm." I kissed his shoulder as he lifted a clump of my hair, pushing it behind my ear. "I was a huge Timberlake fan," I said, loving the feel of his fingers in my hair.

He raked his fingers along my scalp, then, as he'd threatened to do, nuzzled my ear. Heat raced to my sex. I ached for him and we'd barely touched.

"Jeez. This shampoo should be marketed as an aphrodisiac." He slid his hand down my side and over my hip, watching my face for any reaction. He whispered close to my ear. "Maybe I could cut a hole in a shoe box and wrap it up as a gift for you. A special surprise."

"If you could find a box large enough." I spread my hands apart showing a ridiculous length.

Blake laughed, his eyes glittering with the sort of heat that scorched. "You called me a sex god earlier."

"I did." I stroked his nipple, then tweaked it, sliding my leg over his thigh.

His eyes grew heavy lidded. "At the risk of ruining my evening, aren't we supposed to be taking it slow?"

"Have I jumped you?"

"That would be my idea of Christmas. But you'd have to be naked. Or maybe wearing crotchless panties and nothing else."

"It's summertime. Lazy days." I drew out the last two words before licking his lip, clamping my teeth on the plumpest part and tugging it. Licking it again to ease the sting.

Blake's heart was beating faster. "Summer is good too. I can think of all kinds of uses for an icy beverage or a pint of ice cream." He swiped his tongue over his lips. I wanted that tongue between my thighs.

"Whipped cream?"

"Honey."

"Melted chocolate." I loved that idea.

"So good." He swallowed hard.

"You know, I think I have a pair of those..."

"What?"

"The panties."

"With you?"

"No. Not proper boating attire."

"I'll get you a pair with a nautical motif," he said, smiling.

"A long thick mast?"

"Such a bad girl. You have the real thing available right here."

"I'm not sure you'll measure up. Better check."

Kissing my way down his jaw to his chin, I explored his throat with my lips and tongue. His dark nipples needed work so I pinched and licked and tweaked until he moaned.

"Please."

"I love it when you beg." I used my teeth on the sensitive nipple, tugging until he tossed back his head.

"Cold weather's coming." He panted. "Might want to head south."

"That was really bad."

"I'm desperate here." He reached to stroke his cock but I pushed his hand away.

"No, no. I'm inspecting the equipment. No tinkering allowed."

"Fuck. Can you start tinkering soon?"

"Mmmm." I hummed against his belly button, then licked along the line of hair that ran from his lower six pack to the long hard cock standing at attention. My mouth watered.

I started with the tip, circling, sucking, exploring the slit.

"Holy fuck. I'm not gonna last if you keep that up."

"Oh, you'll last." I blew on the wet head as I circled the base with my hand. "So thick." If I hadn't already spent months in his bed as a nineteen and twenty-year-old I might have worried.

"You're killin' me."

"More to come. Pun intended." I licked along his large vein then took him into my mouth, almost gagging on his size. Cupping his balls with my other hand I squeezed gently as I opened to take him deep enough to swallow.

"Baby do that again. Fuck, Anya, that's good. Sooo fucking good. Oh... Yes."

Blake fisted a hand in my hair, arching into me, fucking my mouth, still trying to be gentle. He was big and my mouth was stretched to the limit.

He stopped and pulled away, panting. "Baby, I'm gonna go in a minute."

"That's the point."

I sucked his cock back into my mouth, more determined than ever, and in a few strokes he'd tensed, coming down my throat in spasms, crying my name.

"Anya... Oooh." He clutched at the sheets, his face bathed in sweat, his expression blissful.

I loved having Blake at my mercy. Under my power. His breaths were loud pants, his body shining with sweat. I kissed the head of his super-sensitized cock as was rewarded with a final whimper.

He pulled me up his body so I could straddle his waist.

His eyes were slits as a mischievous grin spread across his face. "You're in for it now."

"Aren't we going to cudd... Yikes!"

He yanked me farther up his body until my pussy was over his face. "Hold onto the back of the couch. I'm taking no prisoners."

Blake forced my legs wider and plunged two fingers inside my soaked cunt at the same time sucking my clit into his mouth. He targeted the sensitive spot inside my sex over and over, his mouth making my clit swell and turn so sensitive I couldn't put two words together. "Blake. Yes. More. Harder."

I fucked his fingers as my pussy twitched with electric shocks. He added a third skilled finger, opening and twisting them inside me. "You're wet for me, baby. So wet. Come now,

Empress. Right now." He rubbed both sides of my hood against the swollen clit.

My body exploded, obeying his commands with glorious pulses and raging waves of pleasure. When I calmed, I scooted down, kissing the beautiful man who'd taken me there, then curling up beside him.

We ended up cuddling that night, but in the morning we learned Adagio was returning to the dock a day early as the weather was changing. Victor didn't take chances, not that anyone would have argued. He'd grown up sailing with his father and knew a hell of a lot more about the changeable Bay Area weather than we did.

Blake drove me home to Palo Alto, and after a sweet kiss on my doorstep, I promised once more to come to the recital on Friday.

11

BLAKE

I nudged Little Phil back into his chair. Kids waiting to go on had assigned seats, unless they were already in wheelchairs, then they were in assigned spots marked with gaff tape.

"Sit. Stay."

"I'm not a dog, Mr. Enfield." Little Phil was seven and squirmy.

"Then behave like a dancer and sit quietly and focus. Go over your steps in your head."

"I know my steps."

"How many hops right before the break?"

He hesitated. "Eight?"

"Seven. There's a hold in the middle. Visualize it and think it through."

"Okay. I will."

"Billy..." He'd been rolling by but stopped. I tilted my head toward Little Phil.

"Sure, I'll stay with this bench." Phil was part of our youngest group. Soon to be hip hopping their way into the audience's hearts.

Val and Tory, my recital assistants, busily combed out hair or adjusted costumes. We didn't bother with the kind of costumes most schools used. Sparkly sequins distracted the audience. We didn't use makeup either. The parents, guardians and our other guests preferred it.

Properly fitting and appropriate shoes were of the upmost importance. I'd danced in too many recitals where a young kid would twist an ankle or end up with blisters. I'd arranged a trade-off system with studios in wealthier areas where outgrown shoes in great condition could be handed out to the kids unable to afford them. I personally fitted each child for my own peace of mind. Anya had taught me how much a sharing community of dancers and dance instructors could help a young student who was already struggling to pay for lessons.

When everyone was pretty much set, I asked Tory to open the door and allow in the audience. They'd been lined up for around an hour. I'd built a performance space in the back, kind of a theatre in the round with levels of fold up platforms and folding chairs around three sides. The set up fit around seventy audience members and I was happy to see the seats were filling up quickly.

I didn't sell tickets. These hard working parents and guardians had paid a weekly fee and brought my young students to class on time. I'd told my young charges to thank their caregivers for every minute spent on buses, trains or sitting in horrendous traffic jams to get here as well as every hour their parent spent seated quietly in the waiting area while they took class.

Some of my students had made cards and little presents for their parents and guardians to thank them. Many of the audience members arrived today with flowers or other gifts.

The kids had worked their asses off and deserved some special treatment.

I was surprised to see Gordon had been one of the first in, holding quite a few seats in the bottom row of one of the side sections. Cassie and Dame followed a minute later. I greeted all three.

"Vic and Sloane are driving to the hinterlands to pick up Anya," Dame said, his British accent more noticeable today.

Dame usually worked in the gallery next door while she taught, his overly protective side on turbo these days. He hated when he was apart from the mother of his heir, as he called the kid. He was only half kidding. Dame and Vic both had serious money."

"I gave a drawing lesson to a group of beginners at the studio this morning. Otherwise I would have been here to help."

"Thank you, but we're fine. Only tell you guy not to call Palo Alto the hinterlands if he want to live another day," I suggested. "Anya is fiercely loyal to tree land."

"Facts are facts."

"I'm not arguing." I held out my hands.

Dame glanced down at his phone. "They've just parked in the lot around the corner."

"Mr. Enfield." Tory looked exasperated.

"Coming." I turned back to my friends. "Thanks for showing up today."

"We're huge fans," Cassie teased. "We'll be signing up the new Granger as soon as we can."

"Give the kid a few years at least. I can't choreograph for droolers or crawlers."

"My child will be born walking." Damien looked down his nose at me, an expression he used to use on school bullies to get them to back off. If they didn't he also knew how to throw a punch. Vic too.

"Oh god. I hope not," Cassie laughed and Damien's adoring expression said everything about how much he loved to see her happy.

"If that's the case, then wait till the kid can understand the word *no*."

"*My* child..."

"Would you stop?" Cassie poked him in the side. Even Gordon was laughing. "*Our* child will be exactly what he or she is meant to be, and whatever that is will be perfect." Cassie kissed Damien on the cheek.

"You're superior to me in every way, luv." He kissed her back.

"Don't forget that sentiment when I'm in labor and screaming at you to fuck off, you monster."

"Please. Labor will be..." Her expression told him it was time to shut up.

A soft touch on my arm. A scent I recognized instantly. "Hey. I made it."

"So you did." A vision of Anya holding a baby flashed into my head, but I blinked it away.

Anya glanced around and smiled. "This place is awesome."

"Mr. Enfield!"

"Shit. Gotta go. See you after the show. Please don't disappear. I'll drive you home." I brushed my mouth against hers and took off, not sticking around to see how she'd react.

"I'll be here."

With a wave of thanks toward Vic and Sloane, I headed backstage.

"Little Phil is nervous. He says he's gonna throw up and

the heel on Sylvie's shoe is loose and...and." Billy was as upset as I'd ever seen him.

"One thing at a time."

"I fixed the heel," Val called out.

"Little Phil is feeling better." Tory waved in my direction.

I crouched down beside Billy and placed a calming hand on his shoulder. The kid lived with an elderly grandmother who did everything she could for the young man. But a kid with no male role models was at a disadvantage. "Here's a secret for when you get a little older and found your own start-up company. A competent staff is worth their weight in gold."

"Yeah, but you were out there so long. You're not even in costume."

"I'm not dancing solo this time around."

"What? You always dance."

"Not solo any longer."

"Wait!" Val wheeled over. She preferred using her manual wheelchair at the studio. "You have to dance. Everyone wants to see you dance."

"This year I brought in a ringer."

"What do you mean?"

I turned to see Keith striding through the back door, his body guard holding it open for him.

"Hey, Blay. Wuzzup?" We did the man hug thing, with a hard pound on the back in punctuation.

"Hey, Pop. All's good. Thanks for coming."

"You...you...you got Popup911 to come?" Val's chin was in her lap.

"P... PopUp911?" He shook with excitement.

"We're buds, Billy," I said. His video had a billion hits, partly thanks to my original choreography.

"We're dueling freestyle. Audience gets to pick the winner." Keith said, grinning.

"Whaaat?" All the kids were on their feet now.

"Everybody down. Pop will only dance if you do your best out there, so Gummy Bears, you're up." The younger dancers got to pick their own group names.

Tory and Val helped the squirts line up. I nodded to my usual jockey and the five to seven year old's came out rocking their moves. I was so proud I almost lost my voice cheering at the end.

And that was just the start. I had a couple of promising young ballroom dancing pairs, kids in their teens who'd been together for five years or so and needed to level up, as well as a group of six talented teens and preteens aiming for Broadway and hoping to become triple threats, meaning they could sing, dance and act. I gave them tap, jazz and contemporary lessons, sending them off to other schools for the rest.

My hip hop, krumping group was led by a local I'd hired in. I didn't have enough experience in that area and man, they really surprised everyone with their difficult moves. My tappers were also taught by a specialized teacher. I knew my limitations.

The best part was when our class of alternately abled kids hit the floor. They'd been in some of the other numbers, mixed up with dancers with healthy limbs and bodies, but they'd come to me and asked for their own number. How could I refuse?

I'd choreographed the number to "How it Feels to Fly" because these kids could teach us all a thing or two about joy and hope and living in the moment. At the softer beginning the four dancers in specially designed chairs lined up with Kendra, our one blind student, perched on a platform on the back of Billy's chair and Dwayne, the young man who'd lost his leg because of a car accident, riding behind Sammi on her scooter.

I called this group Dragons: Fierce. Strong. Always airborne.

Choreographing for the Dragons involved teaching them to maneuver the specially designed chairs while performing mostly arm, head and hand motions, everything set to the soaring music of the amazing song. At the end, the entire audience stood up. I'd noticed a couple of photographers with professional equipment earlier and I'd warned them not to use their flash. They'd obeyed the rules and Gordon didn't have to toss them out on their ears. Guess it was handy that Val was dating a big guy who'd perfected his threatening scowl.

Billy stayed out in front to make the next announcement.

"Now Mr. Enfield and his special guest, PopUp911 are gonna blow your minds with some freestyle, like nothin' you've seen before."

I heard a few gasps in the audience but some of the older attendees looked confused.

I let the kids sit on the floor to watch as Keith and I started out dancing the routine I'd choreographed for his music video just to get the audience warmed up. Soon we split, each of us doing something to the music to entertain and hopefully amaze the non-dancers in the audience. I stuck to what I knew, Latin ballroom, jazz and contemporary, throwing in a couple of acrobatic moves that had everyone clapping and cheering. I couldn't remember having that much fun in a long time.

In a surprise move, Keith gave out passes to all the kids and one adult guardian each to come to the taping of his next music video. Apparently, he was shutting down a section of the SF Zoo next month to film and needed a young audience, some of whom would be in the video. They'd have to be on their best behavior, but hey, my students were the bomb.

I got a lot of hugs from grateful parents and guardians as well as a few potential students asking me about my program. I was gonna need another studio if I expanded any more, but that could be a possibility if I had the right staff.

I'd lost sight of Anya during the goodbyes and searched for her in a mild panic. I found her a few minutes later, helping Val and Tory backstage making sure the kids had their personal belongings. Billy spoke to her rapid fire while she worked.

"What did ya think? Wasn't that the coolest thing ever when PopUp came out? I was gonna scream but that wouldn't have been...ya know. It would have been girly."

"Billy. Girls are not the only gender who scream. Humans scream. It's fine in certain circumstances. But I can speak for the audience when I tell you we're grateful you controlled yourself and didn't scream. Your numbers were wonderful. Every one of them. I was so impressed."

He beamed at Anya. "Oh, I talked to Jim, Ms. Vetrova. He likes the same video games as me. He's gonna come over next Saturday and play. Gram is gonna make baked ziti and garlic bread and salad. He likes that."

"Sounds like delicious fun." She patted him on the shoulder. "I'm proud of you for talking to Jim. He was probably lonely."

"Yeah. Maybe. Well, bye. See you Wednesday before my dance class."

Anya waved at his smiling Grandmother who was standing near the doorway. When she turned and saw me, I was awarded a huge grin I wanted to put in a box and stick under my pillow. She was so beautiful. Perfectly at ease like I knew she'd be.

A dance studio is a dancer's natural environment. A home where all your troubles can melt away, where your spirit soars along with your body. Anya would always be a dancer, whether she danced or not. It sang in her heart and her bones. It shone in every motion of her hands, every tilt of her head.

She reached for me.

"I'm sweaty."

"You must have hugged dozens of people. They didn't complain."

"Yeah, but..."

"And how many times have we been sweaty together?"

"Not enough times. Hoping for more of those." She laughed. "Help me get the stragglers out?"

"Sure."

I paid Flip, my incredible DJ, making sure he knew when he was needed again. I used him whenever I worked on choreography with one of my big name clients. When I finally locked the door and closed the blinds, I took my usual tour of the entire studio, checking windows, making sure everything was in place for the cleaning crew that was set to show up in about an hour.

I fiddled with the lights, making sure one section of the floor was bathed in a warm glow. Then I flipped on a slow, sweet number. I faced my partner, my lover, the woman I wanted to spend the rest of my life with and took in a deep breath.

"Dance with me, Anya."

B lake hadn't phrased it as a question and nothing about his gaze could be described as pleading. He knew I liked it when he took charge, only we weren't between the sheets. The last time I'd danced with Blake I'd fallen. On a floor very much like this one.

Only this man wanted me to dance, not so we could win a contest, or so he could shake off his guilt over his sister's accident. Blake wanted me to dance because he believed in his heart it would be a healing experience for me. This dance was for me because he couldn't hide the love in his eyes any more than I could. He would make it wonderful and by taking those few long scary steps into his waiting arms, I would show him I trusted him with my heart as well as my body.

"I love you, Blake Enfield. Just wanted to get that straight right off the bat."

He blinked a few times, his throat sounding a little tight when he spoke. "And here I was expecting a kick in the ass."

"Your ass is in my top three."

"You have a top three?"

"What woman doesn't have a top three?"

To tease me he smoothed his hands over the cheeks in question. "I'd like to shake a little booty over here with you, so..." He crooked his finger. "Let's play."

He waited. Making it my choice, giving me a chance to change my mind. I wanted to run, to jump into his arms and kiss him soundly. But we were playing, in other words this was a seduction in the making. My body was already tingling at the thought of feeling his arms around me.

If I could just manage to dance through one song without feeling awkward. I placed my cane carefully on the floor and out of the way.

One step. Then another few. My limp wasn't anywhere near as obvious as it used to be. Before I knew it, I stood before my partner, keeping my posture straight, gaze on his. He'd be leading, but I wasn't sure what he had in mind. He seemed so much taller.

I glanced at my feet and laughed. Sneakers. I'd always worn heels when I danced with Blake. Low heels were the best I could manage now, only not today. "I foresee a problem."

"We're not dancing ballroom, Empress."

"No?"

"I have something else in mind. Trust me?"

"Yes." I rose up on tip toes to kiss his sweet mouth.

Blake nuzzled into my hair, taking in a deep breath, one hand on my lower back, the other on my nape. "I will love you for all time, Anya Vetrova."

"How about when I'm ninety-five and get my first wrinkles?"

He cradled my face in his hands. "Especially then."

Our kiss held every buried feeling mashed together, feelings we'd carried around but hadn't the words or the courage to share. At least not until today. A touch of regret, a world of hope. Joy. So much joy to have found each other again. Fear too. Fear because who knew if we could make this work?

His playlist continued, one of Vic's popular hits coming next. A love song. Slow and sweet.

Blake held me close enough to feel every hard muscle of his perfect body, his scent stroking my libido with feather light touches. We swayed like two teens at a high school dance, my body responding to the rhythm slowly at first, then relaxing into Blake's strong lead.

"That's it. You know what to do." He lifted me straight off the ground, his hands at my waist, his powerful arm muscles straining since I was giving him no help at all. I slid down the front of his body, stroking his face and chest with my belly, breasts, and hair.

"Again." I whispered.

Our gazes met and this time I jumped up, holding myself in position with straight arms, my hands on his shoulders, my head above his. He turned in place with me holding onto that position with every ounce of determination I could gather. On top of the world, I smiled like one of the Dragons, flying again when I thought I never would.

This was the most elementary style of partnering, but I was with Blake and Blake loved me.

"I'm going to choreograph simple dances for us. I can lift you in all different ways. Your center is strong. No fancy footwork required. Put your feet on mine." He did a quick turn with me pressed against him like velcro.

I giggled "I'm not limber like I used to be."

"Seemed pretty limber the other night."

He squeezed my ass before dipping me backward and kissing me.

When he brought me back up, I was out of breath. "I wish...your apartment was closer."

"I know a place nearby."

"Not a hotel."

"I happen to have an office right here in this building."

"And does this office have a desk?"

"Even better. It has a bed."

It turned out to be a one bedroom cozy space that Val had decorated, since Blake admitted his sister had much better taste. He insisted on undressing me, and I insisted on undressing him, which took a little longer than I thought because we made a point of admiring and kissing each unveiled patch of skin. Finally naked, Blake led me to bed, kissing me passionately, then whispering all the reasons he loved me.

This wasn't play time where we teased and tortured and joked around. Our affections weren't wild or demanding. We spoke from our hearts, my wall crumbling to ash, his joy burrowing into my heart to warm my spirit.

Blake's fingers worked their massaging magic on my scalp and shoulders, my feet and calves. With soft lips he kissed and licked each toe and finger, the inside of my elbows and the backs of my knees. He spent time loving my scars, nuzzling my belly, worshipping my breasts.

I fell into the mood and returned each loving touch, a spurt of possessiveness shocking both of us. I cradled his face and bit his chin. "You're mine now."

He chuckled. "I belong to the Empress Anya. Forever and always."

I was so relaxed and happy from the massage and the gentle character of our touches, I could have gone to sleep without going further, but Blake had other ideas. He kissed my mouth, my throat, my nipples, sucking and nibbling hard enough to arouse me. I grasped his hand and led it down to my sex, then stroked his cock until he'd grown hard and ready. Spooning had always been one of my favorite positions, so as Blake slid on the condom, I turned. He pushed his body flat to mine, his groin pressing against my ass. Lifting my leg, Blake slid into my pussy at an angle perfect for his cock to stroke against my sweet spot.

He didn't pound into me like I usually craved. Instead his strokes were slow, his caresses tender, the words he whispered near my ear words of lasting love. No man had ever made love to me the way Blake did on this night, and my long ago shattered dreams of what love should be transitioned into a solid future with a beautiful man who would love me as I am, as I loved him.

I peaked first, but my body's strong response brought him over seconds later. After he tossed the condom, we cuddled.

"I'm not giving up my cottage or my practice."

"Would I ever ask you to do that? I'll shift my class schedule around and we can live in your town for a couple of nights a week. I might even like it in the sticks."

"Palo Alto is not the sticks."

"The name means tall tree. How can that not be the sticks?"

"Stanford University is…"

"I'm only teasing. I'll approach with an open mind. Promise." As I rested my head on his chest, he rubbed my back. "I run a dance camp in July but I'm closing the studio in August. Can you get any time off? Hawaii is calling our name."

"Sounds lovely. I'll let my clients know."

"And in the fall…"

He'd left the question hanging in the air.

"Gummy bear dance classes?" I asked. "It'll have to be Fridays or Saturdays. And no classes Sundays. I need at least one day off."

"Fridays at three thirty and another group at four thirty. And maybe contemporary or jazz for the malt balls on Saturday mornings at eleven? They're my eight to eleven year old's. I have a tap and a hip hop instructor come in on Saturday afternoons."

"Really? They picked the malt balls?"

"They thought they were being funny. I made them keep the name even though they wanted to get rid of it a month later. Right after the holiday recital every group gets to vote on different names. All except the dragons."

"You don't take any of your dancers to competitions?"

"No, I've grown to hate that vibe, although I teach serious ballroom to anyone in the teen group who's interested."

"You have two pairs with real potential."

"They have outside coaches who've watched my class and agreed they should continue. I've talked to their parents about what that life entails. I'll help in any way I can, but I'm no coach. You, on the other hand…"

"No. Coaching would take me away from you and my clients. Definitely not worth it."

He pressed his forehead against mine. "Looks like we have a plan."

"I'm planning to sleep until eleven at least."

"I'll be quiet when I get up."

"Are you going out?" I asked.

"Just to get breakfast. Still like chai lattes?"

"Mmm hmm." My eyes were beginning to droop.

He kissed my nose and closed his eyes. "I love you."

"I love you too."

A perfect ending to an incredible day.

13

BLAKE

Holiday recital season was chaotic at the best of times. This wasn't the best of times.

Even though the birth of Penelope Rose Granger had been normal on all fronts, Cassie had gone into labor three weeks early, throwing Damien's plans to enjoy *a few more weeks of restful silence* down the crapper.

Cassie was taking it as well as a new mother with a sulky husband and a baby who slept two hours at a time could manage, but as he was driving the Graham Gallery staff crazy, she often sent him to my studio to see if he could *help* with anything. After taking one look at the circles under his eyes and the disheveled state of his usually pristine clothing, I gave him the key to my upstairs office and told him to feel free to use the shower and sleep on the couch. The bed was off limits. Damien smiled gratefully and did as ordered.

He started showing up around noon every other day. The students announced his arrival and called him *that grumpy guy*.

Cassie asked me one day what miracle I'd worked

because Damien was always in a much better mood when he came home from his visits with me, even taking over baby duties so she could rest. I was sworn to secrecy and told her I wasn't sure what brought on the change.

Anya, not being sworn to secrecy, would probably rat him out if Cassie asked. She and Sloane took turns bringing unneeded food to the Marin mansion - which employed a perfectly good cook - so they could ooh and aah at little Penelope, or Penny, as she was called by everyone except Damien.

"What was the purpose of giving her the Granger family name of Penelope if no one is going to use it?" he complained.

On top of that, one of Anya's clients had shown up at her office with a black eye, so Anya spent that day and the next taking her to the clinic to check for other injuries and file a report with the police, then helping her get a restraining order for the woman's boyfriend. The holidays were one of the police department's busiest seasons, and many of the officers looked overworked.

But for us together, life was perfect. As I'd guessed, Anya was a natural with the Gummy Bears and Malt Balls, keeping them in line with only a glance, yet encouraging their progress with all the right words of praise. They adored her and her class size doubled in a few weeks. It got to the point where I had to hire in one of my teen dancers to help out and shut down registration, something I hated doing. Kids who wanted to dance, should all have the opportunity.

I was toying with the idea of opening up a second studio, but I hated not being able to split myself in half to oversee both. And I definitely didn't want to send Anya to run the other studio. I wanted to keep her right here with me. Especially now.

Our holiday season dress rehearsal ran smoothly, with only a few bits to straighten out. At the end, I gathered up my courage as well as all the teachers and students and assistants, thanked them for all their hard work, then fell to one knee in front of the only woman I would ever love. Had ever loved for as long as I'd understood what love meant.

She was gonna hate that I did this in front of the whole school, but they were my dancing family. Hers now too. Precious in a way only someone who grew up dancing could understand.

She was so shocked to see me on my knee, she wobbled precariously. Val took her hand and placed it on the back of her chair. "It's okay, Anya. It's only marriage. No biggie." I gave my sister a dirty look for jumping the fence and blabbing. She shook her head, laughing. "Like she couldn't figure that out."

The kids were laughing too.

I held out my hands to calm them down. "Give me a break here. This is a first and only time for me." The little ones nodded with big eyes while the older kids rolled their eyes. One of the ballroom partners put their arms around each other.

"Anya, you are my soul, my heart, the love of my life. I want to dance with you forever, share a life, make babies and watch them grow." A few giggles were heard but someone shushed them. "If you'll take me, craziness and all, I promise to love you with every bit of my soul. Please say yes."

"Say yes," Billy shouted, only to be shushed again.

She was on the verge of laughing, although a couple of

tears had beaten a path over her cheeks. "Yes, you silly oaf. Of course I'll marry you. How can I refuse those beautiful puppy dog eyes. Now get up so I can kiss you and the kids can leave. They have a busy day tomorrow."

I rose slowly, narrowing my eyes. I'd get her back. I reached for Anya's waist, yanked her against my body and kissed her for all I was worth. Might as well give them a show. At the end I dipped her back, receiving a round of applause. When I pulled her back up, I slid the sapphire ring Sloane and Val had helped me pick out onto her finger.

Anya looked incredulous. "It's beautiful."

I might not be a member of the B club, but I rested securely in the mid M's.

The crowd congratulated, hugged and kissed us, excited to tell their friends and parents the news. When the craziness ended, the older students went right to work helping prepare the backstage area and dressing room for tomorrow's show. I glowed with pride.

"You've created this amazing community of dancers. There's love here. And respect. And encouragement a lot of these children never receive anywhere else. The teachers feed off your energy and pass it on to the kids."

"Sounds like a bunch of vampires."

Someone clapped from the corner of the room. We turned. Damien leaned against the doorframe, his smile warm and genuine. He must have showered after his nap because his hair was still damp.

He moved forward in three long strides and shook my hand, then kissed Anya on the cheek. "Congratulations. Welcome to the family, Anya."

"The family?"

"Blake has always been family," he explained.

"Thanks. Since you're here, I was wondering... When are you going to open the Gate Club to women?"

"You've been speaking to Sloane I suppose."

"Yes. Enlightening to say the least."

"Between running her restaurant and the Save the Mission crusade I don't know how she finds time for anything else."

"Cassie's on the committee to allow women at the Gate Club too, right?"

"My darling wife is indeed on that committee. Vic and I are doing our best to finalize plans, but it's going to take some time. We'll have to build separate facilities, poll members for their feedback, add another restaurant, expand the pool. It's not a small project and will require a large financial investment."

"According to Blake, a drop in the bucket."

"I beg your pardon?"

"I never said..." Blake held up his hands.

"You said Damien and Vic have multiple B's."

Damien laughed, turning to me. "Wasn't that lawyer-client privilege?" He glanced again at Anya. "He still represents the company I've founded with Vic."

"I think the amount was in Forbes," I said.

"Oh. Well. We always believe what we read in magazines, don't we?" Damien said dryly.

"Recently, Sloane suggested her group hold another rally on the grounds of the club. A get-off-your-asses-and-hire-a-construction-company kind of rally. I'll be attending."

"Looking forward to it."

"Your daughter too, I believe."

"What?"

"A child is never too young to get involved in fighting for

a great cause. Plus, you have a nursery in the building with nannies."

I wrapped an arm around my fiancé, smiling at my long time friend. "She's gonna fit right in."

"You are indeed the perfect pair." I wasn't sure if that was a complement or a criticism.

"Indeed," I echoed, taking Anya's cane and handing it to Damien so I could kiss her thoroughly. When we pulled apart, laughing, Damien had left, leaving the cane leaning against the wall.

"Do you think I pissed him off?" Anya asked.

"Damien and Victor will take their time, but the changes will come. Victor would do anything for Sloane."

"I like being part of a family. I love being part of your family."

"Everyone loves you already." Another kiss. Then another. "Are you tired or would you like to go out? Your choice, Empress."

Anya keyed up a playlist, then lifted her arms. "Dance with me. Help me fly."

She leapt into my arms and I twirled us around until we were both flying.

And I knew, with Anya, I'd be flying for the rest of my life.

THANK you for reading *Split* - The Gate Series Book 3. If you haven't read *Stroke* – book 1 in the Gate Series - check out Damien and Cassie's story.

https://www.mariebooth.com/contemporary

If you'd like to learn more about my Contemporary and Paranormal Romance novels please consider signing up for my newsletter. http://eepurl.com/cLWAmD

Check out my other books here: https://www.mariebooth.com

http://www.bookbub.com/authors/marie-booth

http://www.facebook.com/marieboothbooks

http://www.twitter.com/marieboothbooks

http://www.instagram.com/marieboothauthor

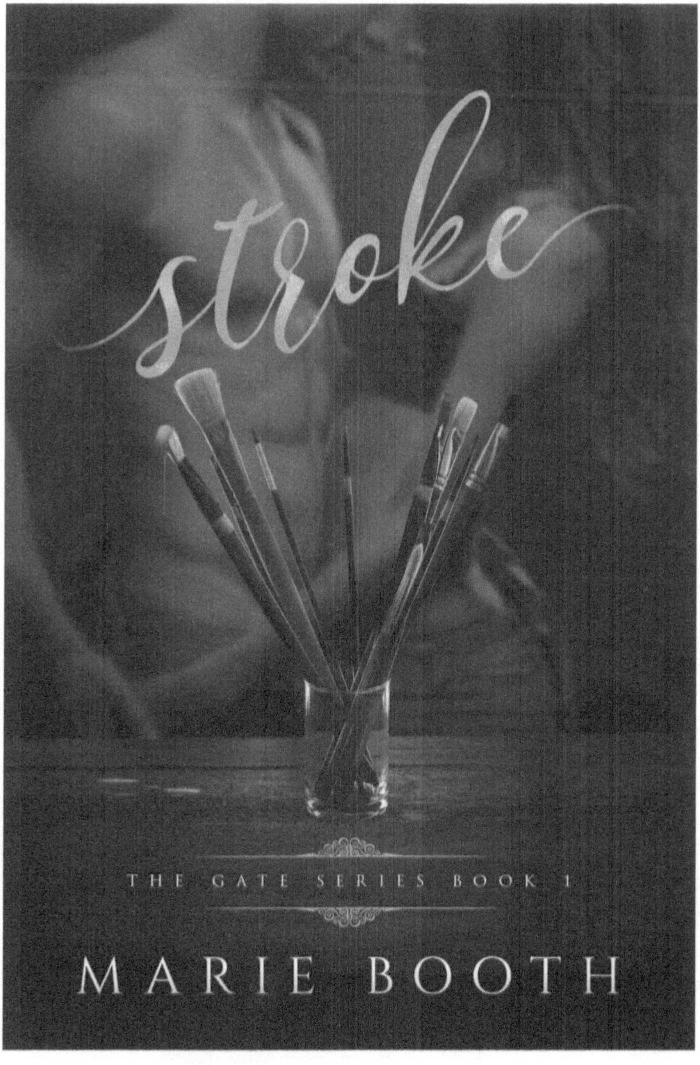
stroke
THE GATE SERIES BOOK 1
MARIE BOOTH

EXCERPT FROM STROKE

THE GATE SERIES BOOK 1

I put aside my latest canvas and rinsed the paintbrushes, swishing them around in the solution I'd developed, then drying each one with extra care. Opening the airing case, I fit them gently into their slots in size order. The paints had already been stowed on the shelves of the closet from whites to pales to pastels, all the way to the richest and darkest hues. It gave me a warm sense of pleasure to look around and see that the equipment I relied on was clean and organized even though my life was a crazy mess.

Passing the full-length mirror, I ground to a halt. The chaos extended to my appearance. Just about every inch of exposed skin displayed colorful blotches and dots. It amazed me that I could make such a mess painting a portrait. I hadn't exactly been delving into the realm of Jackson Pollock.

Despite the bedlam, I was in a good mood. I'd made real progress today. The piece was coming along beautifully, exactly as I'd hoped. I'd be calling my client's secretary within the week. He'd be pleased I'd finished so early and I'd be pleased to get the check.

My assistant, Pam, had plastered a neon pink sticky note on the top right corner of the full-length mirror, her very civilized way of slapping me upside the head to get my attention.

Feb. 15 8:30 p.m. Granger

I glanced at the wall clock. *Shit!* A prospective client was due in less than thirty minutes. *Double shit!* Why hadn't I kept an eye on the time? In a slop sink frenzy, I scrubbed the paint from my hands, fingernails, and forearms with a nail-brush and a good dose of skin cleanser, using a washcloth on my face. I scooped up a clean towel—at least I hoped it was clean—then darted behind the screen and wriggled out of my paint splattered sweatpants and tee, some of the navy blue, cinnamon, and plum paint splotches were still damp. As I pulled on my one pair of decent jeans, I heard foot-steps, heavier and longer than Pam's usual stride. The new client could NOT be early. Not today. Not now. *Please.*

"Hello?" A man's deep voice echoed around the high ceilinged space.

"*Shit!*" Burying my mouth in my palm, I winced. *Great first impression, Cassie.*

A moment of silence. "Are you the art restorer?" He sounded amused. Wonderful. He also sounded British, which made his amusement even more annoying. Americans had nothing on Brits for dishing out scathing remarks, usually delivered in a tone sexy enough to heat my overactive libido.

"Art conservator. Are you Mr. Granger?"

"Yes." The sound of leather soles on the polished wooden stairs told me he was now officially in my studio and I was half naked behind a thin screen. *Fuck!* Where had I left my bra? I never wore it when I painted.

"Just a moment please."

"Take all the time you need. I'm enjoying the build up."

Oh yes, he's laughing at me. But that voice. I could orgasm just listening to this guy. How many times had I swooned over Mr. Darcy? Way too many. I needed a male of the flesh and blood variety to get me off. Only how likely was that to happen? I spent practically every working hour in my studio, splattered with paint or smelling like cleaning solvent.

My luck, Mr. Granger probably looked nothing like Mr. Darcy, the object of many of my fantasies. Cursing quietly under my breath, I toed the clothes on the floor. Where the hell had I left it? I shook my paint-smeared sweats and tee, but nothing. Damn it! I couldn't hold a conversation from behind a screen like the freakin' Wizard of Oz. *Pay no attention to the neurotic artist behind the screen. She's lost her mind along with her lingerie.*

The new client wasn't going to stand around and wait forever and I desperately needed the work. Left without options, I slipped on my cotton pullover sweater and stepped boldly around the edge of the screen and into the room, raking at my hair with clawed fingers. Two feet in, I stopped. Dead.

Danger had strolled into my studio—clothed like a model, built like a god and sounding of sex. I painted sensual portraits and never used models. Instead I observed and took notes or photographs when someone's expression spoke to my artist's soul. My work was erotic and posing models in positions where they felt uncomfortable only produced paintings of uncomfortable models.

Like the famous painting of Count Kochubey by Francois Gerard, Mister Granger was more sensual fully dressed than most men were bare-assed naked. As usual, the first thing I noticed were his eyes, large and nestled beneath arrogant brows, his gaze lit up with a dark amusement at my expense. His styled chestnut hair was windblown, his cheeks still ruddy from the cold.

My body trembled with excitement as I inched closer to my sketchpad. Lovely hazel green eyes. I could work with hazel. Would he allow me to photograph him?

"Are you Ms. Strand?"

My tantalizing fantasy did a drop and roll. "Yes, I'm the owner. I apologize for not being ready on time." The clock read eight fifteen. Okaaay. "As it happens, you are *ahead* of your scheduled appointment."

"I am."

No apology in his tone. No explanation either.

He turned away, presenting me with his back as he scrutinized one of my more generic paintings. A landscape I'd done years ago. For obvious reasons none of my erotic works were displayed. My conservative mother and sister tended to pop in without warning, so I kept my passion for erotic art under wraps, painting under a pseudonym and selling to a private collector.

"I painted that landscape in college."

"Apparently."

Jerk. It wasn't that bad, was it? I hadn't looked at it for a while. I squinted. Yeah, maybe it was that bad. He'd moved on to another painting, so I took a moment to check him out. Early thirties. Tall, maybe six three. Broad shoulders. Long legs. I swallowed hard. Awesome ass. Really Awesome Ass. He must work out.

He'd draped the jacket of his dark gray suit over a wooden chair. I winced, praying this morning's paint spill had dried. The good news? With him turned away, I could view his shoulders and back and Really Awesome Ass without anything blocking my view. His lines were an artist's dream. A thirty year old woman's dream too.

"This one is quite good." He was viewing a portrait of my sister and four-year-old niece as they walked hand in hand on the beach in Monterey, California.

Mr. Granger had shifted his stance. He was right. The view was so very good.

"That's one of my favorites." He wasn't facing in my direction so I snuck over to the closet where I left extra clothes. I must have an old beat up bra as a back up, right? I shuffled a few towels and tee shirts around on the shelves. No luck.

"You've captured the child's expression perfectly."

"Thank you." He must know something about art. "I understand you might need my services?" *Ugh.* That didn't sound right. Initial interviews with clients were usually taken care of by Pam. I was a social disaster.

He'd turned, watching me now, smiling one of those half smiles/half smirks that made me think Hollywood Bad Boy, or maybe Ridiculously Wealthy Rock Star. I glanced toward the entrance and frowned. Hadn't Pam gone home an hour ago? "How did you get in?"

"The door was open."

"No. My assistant locked up." She was very responsible.

"As you see, I'm here." He spread his hands, widening his stance at the same time, taking up more of my territory with his gorgeous body.

"Apparently." I'd meant the word to sound the same as when he'd said it, but my voice had come out strangely husky. His organic scent tickled my nose, a minty cypress with a dash of alpha male—pleasing and provoking at the same time.

My experience with men was limited, so I had few worries he'd be interested in more than a business arrangement. Males of his type would want a woman who knew a hundred ways how to pleasure a man. I was expert in painting a man in the throes of passion. Not quite the same thing, although some of my work could rival the more well known modern erotic artists. Of course I'd never know for sure, as I didn't have the funds or the courage to show my work to the public.

Thank god for my private client. He paid on delivery.

Another delicious whiff of the yummy Mr. Granger urged me toward my desk, my fingers itching to grab up my sketchpad no matter what the purpose of his visit. And what was up with that? Pam usually told me ahead of time what a client was looking for, but the pink sticky had been detail free.

"Why are you here, Mr. Granger?"

When I turned to face him, I was shocked to find he was suddenly close. Too close for a woman who'd gone so long without male attention. Had he countered my steps, moving forward as I'd moved away, or would this man be way too close even if he stood at the opposite end of the room?

He glanced at his diamond studded watch, a languid smile that darkened his eyes accompanying his soft chuckle. "You're working very late, Ms. Strand. I believe eight thirty is no longer classified as evening. It's full night. Aren't you nervous about being alone with the door unlocked?"

Something about his sexy voice, the way it vibrated in sonorous tones deep inside my belly, had me leaning forward. I opened my mouth to respond, but he was already on the move again, strolling around the room with an easy grace, examining the shelves of equipment I used for reparations and the personal items I left on display to add a touch of home.

Before I could stop him he'd picked up a picture of Graham and me. Graham was smiling at the camera with a toothy grin, a bottle of beer in his hand. I was leaning against my little brother, happy and confident. We'd been celebrating our new partnership and the purchase of the studio. He'd dealt with the business end, and I took care of the *artsy-fartsy* stuff – that's what he'd called it.

"This isn't unusually late for me. I find I work better on peaceful nights." Thoughts of Graham had sent a twinge of pain to my heart. "Please." I plucked the picture from his hand and set it carefully in its usual spot on the shelf near my desk, tidying some of the scattered papers while I was at it. Bills, mostly. Graham hadn't been all that great with the business end of things.

Mr. Granger's smoky gaze took me in from my splattered sneakers to my uncombed hair. "I'd apologize—" he nodded toward the picture, "—but I rather enjoy handling things. I'm a tactile bloke."

He'd spoken so softly I almost hadn't heard him, but the effect was instantaneous. The hairs on my arms had taken on a life of their own, my skin prickling with curiosity and yearning. Despite the fact I wasn't wearing a bra, my breasts felt too tight, my hardened nipples chaffing on the weave of the sweater. Attempting to swallow, I found my saliva had deserted me along with my common sense.

His fingers were long and elegant, perfect for all kinds of sensory activities. I fisted my hands and looked away. I had to gain control of this meeting. "I have another appointment this evening." Not bad. Better than *your sexy British accent is making me horny.* "I can give you another five minutes. Please tell me why you made an appointment."

He stared at me and winced. I stepped back, but he stopped me with a gesture, touching a strand of my hair, pulling it toward him and picking out two small dots of plum paint. He held them in the flat of his palm. "It appears you had quite the passionate session with your paints tonight."

As my face heated, Mr. Granger flicked the paint off his hand and into the wastebasket beside my desk, then allowed my hair to slide through his fingers until it rested again on my shoulder. He smiled, one brow rising slightly higher than the other—a modern version of a Regency rake. "I wasn't aware you painted."

Painted? A simple word for an agonizing, frustrating, glorious process. My current study of a young man and woman had obsessed me to the point of losing sleep. It was commissioned and due to be delivered to my private collector in one month's time. I'd been fortunate to find a sponsor, as restoration work was slow and his or her generous payments were keeping a roof over my head and food on the table.

Mr. Granger was striding toward my latest painting. No one was allowed to see my work before I deemed it finished. "Mr. Granger, you still haven't told me why you've come." I motioned for him to move toward the entrance where we could sit and discuss business more comfortably.

He returned his attention to me, but didn't move. "I have a proposition that might interest you, but I'll need some time to explain the situation. Have you eaten?" He slipped on his dark gray suit jacket, adjusting it to hang perfectly. He buttoned the top two buttons and I had to force myself to look away. It had been over a year since a flesh and bone male had touched me, but this guy was so out of my class.

"I'm sorry, but..." I sensed motion out of the corner of my eye and glanced down. *Oh god.*

My wayward bra lay in a sad heap on the floor by Mr.

Granger's feet, the contrast between the ratty gray cotton fabric and his perfectly shined five hundred dollar Italian leather shoes was almost ridiculous enough to make me laugh. Almost. Instead my face heated to steel melting temperatures. The bra had slipped off the chair when he'd removed his jacket.

He stooped to pick it up before I had the chance to move. "Were you looking for this?" He dangled the comfortable and inexpensive bra from his large hand and I reached for it, my movements seeming to slow as I accidentally brushed several of his long fingers with my own. My body tingled, blood flowed to my lower belly.

I'd never experienced this kind of instant lust before. I skimmed his body with my gaze then lifted my head to meet my prospective client's eyes. Mr. Granger was feelin' it too.

Bunching my bra, I shoved it into my pocket and forced a smile. My face had warmed but I wasn't sure if it was because I'd left the bra displayed on the chair in the main room or because he'd seen that I wore such unappealing lingerie. I made a note to buy something sexy. You know, just in case.

Mr. Granger leaned several inches closer, his warm breath dusting my cheek. "There's no need to put it on for my benefit, Ms. Strand."

I glanced at my breasts, the current object of his interested gaze. My nipples were poking against the soft cotton, standing at attention like good little soldiers awaiting the general's approval. He was quite taken with them, and the girls had made it clear they were more than excited to be admired by a hot guy. My nape dampened as warmth crept down my neck to spread out across my chest.

Stepping away, I cleared my throat. It seemed I was always in a state of retreat around this man. I backed toward the small restroom. "I... I have a long day ahead of me tomorrow and my next appointment..." Now I was repeating myself. On top of everything else, my stomach picked this moment to rumble loud enough to make his brows rise and his eyes crinkle with humor. Awkward didn't begin to describe it. "Excuse me for a moment, please."

I moved as quickly as I could into the tiny restroom, slipped off the sweater, redressed, and smoothed down my wavy brown hair. Returning to the main room, I found Mr. Granger standing near my latest painting.

My stomach dropped. Too late. "I'm closing up now." I'd added some brusqueness to my tone, but he hadn't gotten to the point of his visit and my time was as valuable as his. I pushed a few papers around on my desk, hiding the rest of the bills.

"My business offer is generous, an opportunity a professional with your talent and understanding of art would not wish to pass up." He smiled, the expression genuine and dazzling. His voice warmed to a more relaxed tone. "You look like you could use a good meal. Maybe a drink as well? Join me for dinner. I made a reservation at Eduardo's near Pier 14 on the Embarcadero. It's not far from your residence and the food is exceptional."

It was true I'd only had fruit for breakfast and crackers and cheese for lunch, but Eduardo's? The average Joe couldn't get a reservation for that restaurant unless they signed over their first-born child along with the neighbor's kid. "How do you know where I live?"

He chuckled. "You'd be surprised at what pops up on the internet."

As he tugged on one of his cuffs, my gaze darted again to the tasteful ring on his pinkie finger. It looked like an antique. "What do you do, Mr. Granger?"

"I acquire art for various clients, some with eclectic tastes. I'm also a collector."

Sounded sort of Bundy/Lector. "What do you collect?" He'd better not say butterflies. Or teeth.

He laughed at my wary expression. "Primarily oil paintings. Sometimes sketches, books, sculpture and antique jewelry. Whatever strikes my fancy." He moved closer to the desk. "You should wear your hair back. Your eyes are lovely." He tucked a clump of hair behind my ear, then frowned, reaching for another strand.

I stepped away. "Mr. Granger..."

"Come to the mirror." The Greek god was giving orders. I shrugged and followed.

He positioned me in front of the glass before lifting a clump of hair from the back of my head. "More paint, I'm afraid. It's quite obvious who won tonight's battle of the brushes. May I?"

I nodded, mesmerized by the view of us together in the full-length mirror—my companion touching my hair, intent on his task, his mouth curling into a sexy curve, his breath teasing the skin of my neck.

"Hold out your hand." I obeyed instantly, not wanting this moment to end. One by one he placed the tiny dots of hardened paint on my palm, sometimes stroking the sensitive skin as he returned for another piece. When he finished, he didn't move away. Like me, he scanned our reflection, his eyes widening, his head tilting.

Although the hand in my hair was our only point of contact, he was so close the heat from his body warmed me from shoulders to thighs, sending tingles along my skin and pleasure to my core. I envisioned the same picture of us in a more sensual setting. We'd be staring at our reflections as we were now, but in a bedroom. I'd be in an open silk robe, naked beneath. He'd wear slacks or jeans, no shirt, his hazel eyes lustful as he imagined all we would do that night.

I shivered, the slight achiness between my thighs a welcome sensation even though I'd find no release with this man. It had been a long time since I'd experienced wanton need—pleasure and pain combined. I toyed with the idea of turning and pulling him closer. Maybe leaning back against his chest, reaching behind me and rubbing his cock until he was ready.

He smiled like the rogue I suspected hid beneath the thousand-dollar suit, "I didn't expect to find you so distracting." He stepped back and half my body warmth retreated with him. "Put on your shoes and tell me where you keep your coat. I'm taking you to dinner."

There was no arguing with that sexy tone, not that I wanted to argue. What I wanted to do was skip dinner, loosen his tie, unbuckle his belt, and slip off his jacket. Discover and explore. He'd glanced at my desk several times. I could easily sweep aside all those papers I'd just straightened. His words struck home and I looked down at my bargain store jeans and sweater. "I'm not dressed for Eduardo's," I whispered, my voice dry and shaky.

"You're with me, Ms. Strand." Spoken as if that would solve everything from world hunger to a particular young woman's sexual needs.

"I'm Cassie."

"Cassandra?"

"I prefer Cassie."

He extended his hand. "Damien."

It seemed silly to shake hands after he'd had his fingers in my hair and his breath on my neck, but I did. Warm and large and long fingered. I smiled as I slipped on my red flats, spinning another fantasy, this time involving those sexy hands. Raking my fingers through my hair one last time, I tumbled the dark waves over my shoulders in a sad attempt to look like I belonged beside a man like Damien Granger.

My coat was a dark scarlet wool and he helped me into it, sliding it onto my shoulders with care. My cardinal lipstick was the only makeup I took the time to apply. I turned away from the mirror and he grinned, a surprisingly boyish expression greeting me.

"Eduardo's may not be ready for you." I smiled at his jibe but was surprised when he held out his hand. "I promise you won't be disappointed."

Stroke is available here and on Kindle Unlimited. Stroke

MARIE BOOTH & HER BOOKS

Marie's a California girl who happily shares her life with two daughters, her very patient older brother, and a big boned solid black rescue cat named Stealth.

Marie's Books:

<u>THE GATE SERIES</u>: A hot contemporary romance series set in the beautiful San Francisco Bay Area.

BOOK 1: **Stroke**

BOOK 2: **Simmer**

BOOK 3: **Split - (A novella)**

BOOK 4: **Snap** releasing soon

<u>**STEAMY BITES SERIES**</u>

BOOK ONE: **Dying for a Bite:** a Small Town RomCom Vampire Ménage

<u>**SANTA CRUZ SHIFTER SERIES**</u>

BOOK ONE: **Flying Hard**

BOOK TWO: Releasing in 2020

<u>THETA SERIES</u>: Urban Fantasy with demons, vampires and a whole new breed of supernatural

BOOK 1: **Playing with Passion**

BOOK 2: **Yielding to Pleasure**

<u>**ROMANTIC & FUNNY SHORT STORIES:**</u>

Ringing in the Reefer - From the *Worst Holiday Ever* anthology set in the **Steamy Bites** world

Love Ya Baby - From the *Worst Valentines Day Ever* anthology, set in **The Gate Series** World

Find out more at http://www.mariebooth.com

If you like paranormal romantic adventures, check out Marie's other persona, Gayle Parness: http://www.gayleparness.com
Rebirth - Rogues Shifter Series Book One - is permanently free at all vendors.
Rebirth